P[illegible]
VIRGINIA HAMILTON'S
Plain City:

★ "Hamilton's style gets plainer, but her words lose none of their music or their depth. She makes one girl's search for identity both a realistic story and a universal myth of awakening."

—*Booklist,* starred review

★ "With exceptional grace and honesty, Hamilton (*M.C. Higgins, the Great; Many Thousand Gone*) sketches a vibrant portrait of a gifted 12-year-old of mixed race in search of her identity....Accented with rivertown dialect, the lyrical narrative will draw readers into the small community of Plain City....Richly textured with a cast of unforgettable characters, this extraordinary novel offers a rare glimpse of unconditional love, family loyalty, and compassion."

—*Publishers Weekly,* starred review

★ "Through candid thoughts, realistic dialogue, and a symbolic blend of setting and self-discovery, Hamilton has created a testimonial on the powerful bonds of blood and 'back time,' or heritage."

—*School Library Journal,* starred review

◆ "Subtle, wise, complex—superb."

—*Kirkus Reviews,* pointed review

“Hamilton writes with her usual grace and perception. *Highly recommended.*”

—*Book Report*

“A rich assemblage of characters . . . memorable.”

—*BCCB*

“This perceptive coming-of-age novel introduces a remarkable heroine in Buhlaire Sims . . . powerfully evocative.”

—*The Horn Book Magazine*

“*Plain City* is the kind of rich, well-written story we have come to expect from Hamilton.”

—*VOYA*

PLAIN CITY

PLAIN CITY

VIRGINIA
HAMILTON

POINT

SCHOLASTIC INC.
New York Toronto London Auckland Sydney
Mexico City New Delhi Hong Kong Buenos Aires

ISBN 0-590-47365-4

14 13 12 11 10 9 8 7 2 3/0

Printed in the U.S.A. 01

Author photo by Jimmy Byrge

For Bonfire

PLAIN CITY

1

Buhlaire

You all don't scare me. Snap! She elbowed the two older students to one side of the icy walk.

"It's that Water House child," one of them spoke low to the other as Buhlaire burst past them.

They clutched their bookbags. Whispered about her. She made them look where they were going. They thought where she lived told on her, or so she believed.

She took long, rushing strides. She glanced back at them over her shoulder. Giggled when they wouldn't look her in the eye. But inside, she wasn't laughing. She felt everybody was always looking at her. *Taking all the space on the sidewalk — who do you think you are? — shoot.*

Buhlaire was a going-on-thirteen image of slim and tall Bluezy Sims, her almost-thirty-year-old mom. Her hair was straw-colored, made even lighter by last summer's sun. Most of the time she wore it "out," unbraided. Summer or winter, her hair rimmed her heart-shaped face in golden Rasta twists. Even in the bitterest cold, nothing and nobody could make Buhlaire wear a hat.

After a rain, or in fog or snow, her eyes were the shade of first light with glowing tones of sun-up. Usually her eyes were gray or blue-green. And they could pick up other pale colors from the sky. Summers, she peeled her clothes off down to the barest decency. She tanned to near-chocolate lightly washed in burnt orange.

Summer coming's going to be a good time, shoot. Buhlaire felt it inside. Every season was a chance for changes. *It's after the holidays. And snap! School-up again. Maybe something different will happen for the new year. Something good. Things have got to change. Snap!*

Winter's not too uncool, either. I can handle it. Through the long winter, her skin never lost its carrot-honey tinge from the summer's sun. It was a glowing reminder of good things to come.

Winter'll be over some day. Started out dry cold. Thirty degrees all through Christmastime. Be brittle cold out now. January, but I like this day, about to break up into teeny, tiny ice stars.

On the real cold days, she wore her white wool jumpsuit Bluezy and Aunt Digna bought her for Christmas. It was the same glowing white as the snow in sunshine. She had on white fake-fur-lined rubber boots with high-top leather shoes on inside them, and wool socks inside *them*. She wore white wool gloves.

At first glance, Buhlaire was invisible from the neck down. Moving quietly in the out-of-doors, her head seemed to float on air. Around her carrot-honey face was that fuzzy-gold halo of Rasta hair. She looked like a sunflower, lost its stem.

Buhlaire could startle. It took a few seconds to see all of her in her snowy getup.

She wore the jumpsuit to school practically every day. Sparkling clean at first, it got dirtier by the hour — dust, soot, colored chalk. Easy to see in the classroom how young she was. Her yellow mop-head was stuck there atop a long, lanky shape.

After school, she never could stay in one place for long. Buhlaire saw kids she knew sledding in Montgomery Park. But going up and down the few medium-high hills on a sled, with a bunch of her classmates, couldn't take her where she wanted to go. Besides, she didn't own a sled.

Mom: "You're too old for that kind of stuff. You want to break some of your bones? Sledding's for little kids."

Her mom didn't know any better. Kids Buhlaire's age were into all kinds of serious mischief. They acted as if they didn't want her around. *By myself is best; go where I want. Get going. Winter won't give me much time before the sun sets. Maybe some three hours.*

Buhlaire was on the move, tramping through the snow. She knew Plain City mostly by walking it. She strode through the Uptown area, which bordered the Midway section where the school campus was. She kept her head down, watching her feet, and tried not to stare at the grand houses that stood like great boxes three stories tall. She caught a glimpse of their snow-covered lawns as she quickly passed through to the other side of the Jacoby Hill.

There, she got on a bus before anyone had time to wonder what business she had on a blustery, snow-drifting day up in that part of town.

I got plans, just as soon as it's warm.

She left the bus in Midway and walked quickly down the avenue. She stared into the flower shop and the jewelry store windows. There were lots of businesses. Around the corner there was a hostelry called "Shelter . . ." in big red letters, followed by "From *Any* Storm" in green neon. Mostly people who had no place else to live stayed there. The name of it always made her smile.

She went in Vinda's Donut Shoppe to get warm. Little tables were set out in front of glass counters of pastry. Buhlaire stayed to have a hot chocolate.

Customers and the waitress gave her hard glances. But she didn't let on that the stares bothered her. She had her school books with her and pretended to read. But she was watching her hands and warming them around the cocoa mug. Their looks spoke to her: *Stay in your own part of town.*

'Cause of Mom? 'Cause I'm a Water House kid? Both? She guessed that they made comments about her after she left. Made up their minds about her.

A classmate's mom had already decided who she was: "Some left-over sixties flower child, took a wrong turn down the highway to Plain City."

It got back to Buhlaire by way of an almost-friend named Sandy Brown, the principal's daughter. Jamie Fugate's mom had said it. And said she didn't want Jamie "hanging" with Buhlaire at the mall. "You can't help talking to her in school," Jamie's mom told Jamie. Jamie had clued Sandy, and Sandy had passed it along to Buhlaire.

Probably some more Sandy wouldn't tell me. The mom saying stuff like, "You come in contact with her playing basketball, all right. But any time outside of sports and school, you stay away from that Water House girl, hear?"

All the time making things up about me, dissing me like that. Just disrespectful. It puzzled Buhlaire why people did that.

"They think they know me," she'd told Sandy Brown.

"Buhlaire, if you'd just not act like you think you're better'n everybody — just to act normal, and like you cared about something half the time — people would forget what you look like." Sandy sucked in her breath. She'd blurted out the last part before she'd thought. She hurried off with her friends.

Buhlaire had rushed to the restroom the first chance she'd gotten. Peered in the mirror again to see what she must look like to everybody. She had no idea what she looked like outside herself, to people. She knew all the parts, but she couldn't place them in any kind of order that was Buhlaire. Each time she looked in a mirror, it was as if she saw this person she didn't know and never expected to see.

I don't think I'm better'n everybody. Why'd she say that? I look freaky? I sure don't look like anybody else, not even my mom. Why! Phooey. I could reverse-perm my hair, make it lay down. Why! Why should I bother about it?

But it had startled her, the last thing Sandy had said.

Think I'll tell her she should hang with me one day, see what I have to put up with every time I go anywhere in Midway. Storepeople, following me around. They don't do that to any other girl. Buhlaire was convinced of it.

She didn't think she was a flower child. She knew about sixties clothes. She knew about the war. Her dad was missing from it, wasn't he?

Half the kids in school had dads not at home. A few had missing moms. Most were missing dads, who had divorced *them*. That's the way the kids felt. Not "My mom and dad are divorced," but "My mom and dad divorced *us*." That was the way Buhlaire felt, too.

But none of the kids had a war and missing in action like she had with her dad. *War sounds more of a mystery. Not that Saudi Gulf War, either, but Nam. Nam was a real war.*

It made her proud to be able to say, "It's because of Nam, my dad is missing." She'd been told that a long time ago, probably by Aunt Digna, who was her dad's sister. Her mom never said much that you could count on about her dad or anything else. "*We don't see him around town, do we?*" Bluezy saying, all gloomy and tired.

"*I've never seen him around anywhere,*" Buhlaire went.

"*Then you could say he's missing.*" And her mom had shut up about it.

Buhlaire didn't let herself think much on the subject. She didn't want to believe her mom was cold, so she didn't ask anymore. But something came to her one day when they studied the Green Mountain Boys, and the American Minutemen of 1776.

I've got no back time, hardly. Been born, been an American, but twelve years. I'm not even thirteen. Mom and Aunt Digna never tell me of their back time. They say I wouldn't find it interesting. They just grew up, that's all. Which leaves me thinking, all of us are just here and now. Nothing ever was of us before, in some long, way-back time.

Sandy saying, "Buhlaire, you better not talk too loud about your dad and Nam. 'Cause it doesn't figure."

"What's that suppose to mean?" she'd said, all in a huff at Sandy.

"Oh, kid, just shut up about it!" Sandy came back, sounding all big and tired of Buhlaire. As though she'd meant to say, "*Well, what can you expect from a Water House kid?*" It made Buhlaire feel small.

In twenty minutes, she was warmed inside by the cocoa. Then she left Vinda's Donut Shoppe. Outside, she was soon tramping mostly unseen along the length of the Montgomery Falls River.

Early January, and the temperature stayed below freezing. The river water was frozen solid. Six inches of powdery snow lay on top. Buhlaire trudged along right on the ice, making snow tracks.

I'm walking on water, too — holy, holy. Snap! Second year in a row. Not every year would it stay cold long enough for ice to form on the river.

She tramped in the snow until she had to stop to get her breath. Then, she got down on her knees. Brushed the powdery snow away and smoothed her gloved hands on the ice. She stretched out on her stomach and stared down into the under ice, to see what she could see.

Hunh. It's all black ice in there, seems like. Fishes, living down there, I'll bet, while everything up here is freezing. She thought she saw shapes way deep down there. Eyes and noses. She lay like that for a while, feeling the cold all around, pressing down on her from the trees hanging over her. She had her nose flattened against the ice, wondering if her skin would stick there. She hoped to see — she didn't know what. Almost scaring herself.

There's nothing to see. Just layers of ice. You can't see through thick ice. Gingerly, she lifted her head, sniffed with her nose.

There was bitter winter wind in the bare branches above her. But it was peaceful on the ice where she was. So very still. She rested her head on her arms.

Now I lay me down . . . It's soooo quiet! 'Cept for the wind, I could fall asleep. She was so comfortable. But slowly the inside of her jumpsuit cooled. The winter wind had penetrated the cotton sweater she wore next to her skin. That meant her body would start its cooling off, too.

As long as Buhlaire moved, she stayed warm. *Freeze out here, and I'd look just like part of the snow. A snow lump, never to be found until spring.*

Oh, but she would be found, as quick as a wink!

She sat up then. *"Don't always act like a child," Aunt Digna says.* Buhlaire smiled, knowing she was too old to be lying on her stomach in the dead of winter, looking for fishes. She got to her feet and wiped the flaky snow off. She walked, keeping her mind a blank, keeping back feelings. *Why do I hold myself so tight in?* She didn't let out any answer.

She was not alone. There was someone with her who thought she was amazing. She knew that much. *What's he think when I lie on the ice? Thinks I'm crazy!* He never came close to her, but stayed out of sight. And yet, he followed her. She knew it was him. Started following her as soon as the snow fell and she began tramping out. A week and a half? Maybe longer.

Knowing he was watching made her feel creepy sometimes. But she cut that out, too. Other times, she was glad to know he was there. She could hear him, when she stepped suddenly, catching him off guard. Then, she would smile to herself. She never turned around to see. That would be like cheating, somehow. It was some kind of game; win or lose, she would play it out.

Sometimes Buhlaire thought she could hear him

breathing, he would be that close. *Never thought any boy like him ever'd come so close. Maybe it's my mind playing tricks. A little scary out here.*

When she was a couple of miles on the outskirts of town along Jacoby Road, she was glad to have company of sorts. Out where she could see the cars on the interstate sweeping by Plain City. It was as if they ran on a track on the winter plain that went straight and flat for miles. Cars and trucks, in a steady swooshing noise, going places. They left Plain City behind in the cold.

Out here there were enough trees so that the two of them never saw each other. *But I know he knows I know he's there.*

Grady Terrell. Just the nicest-looking boy; the biggest kid in her homeroom.

Out here, he watches my back. He's just afraid to show he likes me. In school, he is the worst kind of nothing.

Aunt Digna goes, "Buhlaire, you'll learn the hard way. A young girl should not be biking by herself."

I sure told her, too: "I wish you all would quit spying on me!"

And all wrong, thinking bad things, Aunt Digna goes, "Buhlaire, are you out there with some boy?"

"No, Aunt Digna!" Why she has to insult me like that! Shoot, so I sass her, "You're not my mom. And anyway, I know my way around. I know every rock, tree, and building. Nobody but me bikes." Lying. "Nobody's going to bother with me, too."

"Until the first time," Aunt Digna goes. "Until one time somebody comes up behind you, and we don't never

hear from some Buhlaire Miz Sims again."

Aunt Digna had looked away when she'd said that. But Buhlaire saw the shining fear in her eyes. The love there. "*Tell your mama, too, if I have to.*" None of them in the Water Houses liked getting Bluezy in a rage.

I go, "Well, go ahead, Aunt Digna. Tell her if you want to. She won't care. She knows I can take care of myself."

Digna, shaking her head, always hoped for the best and expected the worst. She stayed angry at her sister-in-law, Bluezy. Bluezy, putting herself first, above this heartache child, Buhlaire. Leaving Digna in charge of a lonesome, growing pain of trouble.

2

Mellow Yellow

Calling her one of his nicknames again. Calling her Mellow Yellow. *Name comes from an olden song.* He would come up behind her in the hall and sing in her ear, *"They call me Mellow Yellow . . ."* She hated anybody who couldn't carry a tune. She despised somebody laughing at her color.

"Somebody better quit it." She never called Grady Terrell by his name, or spoke to him directly. "I answer to Buhlaire. See if anybody can say it right. B'laire, hard on the *laire*."

He burst out laughing. Then, mocking, "Who-wut? Bull what? Bull Hair?" Just loud so everybody could hear.

Out of school it was follow-the-leader. Across the snowfields, she sensed he cared about her. In school, neither of them let on there was anything but loathing between them.

Did I make it up — him, out there with me? No, he's there, looking out for me? Watching me, anyway.

In school, the sight of her set him off. She'd have to defend herself. In school and outside, he was two different people. So was she.

Grady sat across from her and one seat back in homeroom. She wouldn't look around at him, but she could feel him watching her.

All the time calling in a loud whisper, "Anybody know some Bull Hair Sins around here?" It was his name for her in place of Buhlaire-Marie Sims, her real name. Most people called her Buhlaire. Grady called her Yellow Mellow Halo when he wanted to make a joke about how pale she was with her bushy, straw-carrot Rasta hair.

He hates my hair. My color.

She took his woofing to heart. She wrote on blackboards in homerooms, so everybody could see: "Sicko Grady, the Wart Hog, lives to rut in the Plain City garbage." Their homeroom teacher fussed at all the kids: "Why must you insult one another? Can't you respect one another?"

They heard her. They felt sheepish for a while. But they could not stop the dissing. Disrespect. Woofing back and forth was the way they got along.

Buhlaire planted two notes, one on the floor by Grady's desk and one sticking up out of the snow. Any kid going by could pick one up and shout it around, which was what happened. Everybody dived for notes dropped by mistake or left on purpose, it didn't matter. Then they would spread the news and gossip about whatever it was they'd found out.

"Students, if you cannot think of anything better to do with your time, you might as well not come to school," said their teacher. She sent a steady stream of them to the principal's office.

Buhlaire's note went, "Call some names one more time and the hog's nose gets — pow! — and swollen bigger than it is." But writing tough like that always made her feel funny.

"Buhlaire, that's so mean," Sandy said. "Writing on blackboards and notes and stuff."

"How come you didn't hear what the sicko said to me?"

"He's a stupid *boy*, Buhlaire. I think he likes you. Anyway, he *said* something, he didn't write it *down* for everybody to see."

"What's the difference?" Buhlaire wanted to know.

"Because *he* says it so we'll all laugh and stuff. But you write it to get even. Better should ignore him because you're gonna get in trouble before he does."

For a short minute, Sandy walked down the hall with her, had her hand on Buhlaire's shoulder, too. It was as if Sandy forgot herself, letting her feelings show for Buhlaire. It thrilled Buhlaire to have herself and Sandy behaving just like friends, together.

Buhlaire knew if there was trouble, she'd get in it first. She just seemed to irritate people. But she managed to get the nickname "Sicko" to stick to him. All the kids now said it.

"Well, see ya," Sandy said and spun around, going back the other way to her class.

Like, she can't be around me more than a minute. Afraid what her friends will say, too.

What Buhlaire wrote had hurt Grady Terrell.

Sandy told her things like that in confidence. Said Grady didn't know how to turn it all around. That he often dreamed about Buhlaire. *Wonder what other boy told Sandy that?* And most days, he woke up thinking about Buhlaire. Said he couldn't wait to get to see her. *Even though I'm an "outside" child who looks different, who's got no dad?* She thought Sandy made it up to hurt her. Said Grady thought Buhlaire was the most "other" girl in Plain City.

It was true that Grady seemed not to be able to take his eyes off Buhlaire. With her gold and orange hair and her skin with its orangish glow, she knew she stood out in a crowd of teens. Parents talked about her. That didn't mean they liked her. She got under everybody's skin because of who she was and what she looked like. *Not any one thing. All mixed up. Huh. Outside.*

Out of nowhere, Aunt Digna came floating in her thoughts, saying, "*One of Junior's — vanilla.*" She floated out again before Buhlaire had time to think what that was about.

Buhlaire was right back to Grady. *I still think he half hates me.*

She didn't know how she was supposed to be to anybody and everybody. Nobody at home told her anything about what to do. *Mom goes, "Digna, don't you tell the child how to behave. What is wrong with the way she is? Let all them learn how to behave toward her. Let them change themselves, if changing is in the cards."*

Sicko Grady got away with everything. He acted

normal, which was how he looked. Which meant he knew when to act up and when to listen to authority. He knew how to get along. He was too cute; girls liked him. So did boys. He was bigger than any one of his thirty classmates. That gave him sort of a higher place, Buhlaire felt. An edge she resented.

She figured he picked on her because of who her mom was and where they lived. He lived in the Midway area, way back from the Montgomery Falls River, in a shady-lawn side of the central city. *House has an attached garage, and everything.*

I know his aunt. Once she spoke to me. It was at the mall. I was walking behind a bunch of kids from school. Sandy was with them. And his aunt thought I was with them, too. So she spoke to me. Said, "Hello there, how you doing?"

Buhlaire figured that Grady disliked her because she was the Water House child "with light eyes." *Then why does he like me, too? Why does he follow me?*

Lunchtime. Sitting in the lunchroom at long tables, girls on one side, boys on the other. Or tables pushed together; boys filling one table, girls, another. She was at the end, away from the most popular ones, with the girl seated next to her, turned from her. The girl didn't want to have to look at Buhlaire, or touch her.

They let her sit at the table because Sandy said it was a public school place and she could sit where she liked. They listened to Sandy because she was the principal's daughter. But they moved over as far away from Buhlaire as they could.

"The W.H.C.!" Grady hollered, meaning the Water House child. She knew at once what he meant. She always waited for him to think of a new way to put her down. He leaned around some guys, looking toward her. Everybody turned to stare at her. They got that expression, like she was weird. "No, the W.C.!" Grady said in a loud whisper. "Everybody know what W.C. stands for?"

"The Water Houses, right?" Jason Davis asked.

"E-ooh! E-ooh! The Water Houses!" girls squealed.

"No, it's the W.C., the Water *Closet*. The john!"

"Grady, Sicko, e-oooh!" some girls told him. He didn't like being called Sicko. But since Buhlaire had first called him that, he let it go. When somebody called him Sicko, he would say, as he did now, almost gently, "Bull Hair started that."

He had to go on with it: "My cousin Darrell was stationed overseas, and that's how foreigners call the john. The W.C. Yellow Mellow Halo lives in the W.C.! Haaaah!"

Some kids snickered. "Grady, whyn't you be-*have*," Sandy said mildly.

"Want me to plant your head in the ground?" he answered. Suddenly, he had an older look in his eyes that made Sandy shift uncomfortably in her seat. At once, everybody else seemed to be hard at work eating.

Nobody cares how I feel. Nobody else ever even woofs on me.

She'd heard that Grady was mostly sorry he'd started it. They were only in the seventh grade. Maybe he'd learned hatefulness from uneasy eighth graders, six months away from scary high school.

Some real devilment made him pick on Buhlaire. By himself, he would beat on the walls of the boys' bathroom just to hurt himself. Calling her all those names.

Today she hated him. She could be looking down at her plate, moving food around, but she let him know, and she knew he could tell, that she would just as soon spit on him.

Sicko Grady. I wish, I wish. Dumb, dead Grady . . .

She tended to think she was the one and only Water House kid, although she wasn't. There were six houses. Some of the kids were related to her. Others belonged to the renters. She didn't keep track of any of them much. They weren't like her or her mom. And she was picked on because of that, maybe. Also, because of the way Bluezy behaved with other people, even Aunt Digna. Like, she looked down on you. Like, what she knew and did was so much better.

Her mom, Carmen Bluezette Sims, had *publicity*. Very embarrassing show bills with her picture. The whole head-to-foot of her. Under the picture, in big, bold letters:

CARMEN BLUEZETTE SIMS
SINGER
EC+DYS+I+AST! AND HER FAN-DANCING!
TRUE BLUE "BLUEZY" SIMS
FRI., SAT., SUN., AT DELMORE'S
9 P.M. TO 2 A.M.

Saying, "Mom, can't we move on from here, to where it's bigger and not everybody has to know who we are and what you do for a living?"

"It's a good living, and it's a good base, here."

"But why can't you just sing, and not the rest?"

"There's nothing wrong with what I do. What's wrong is in people's heads. Here is where my property is. And here's where we stay."

Buhlaire got up from the table, pushing back the chair with the backs of her legs. She had her lunch tray in one hand and her half-empty container of chocolate milk in the other. She marched down along the tables, going past the boys' table, to Grady. She squeezed the corner of her tray in next to his. Held it there with one hand. Swiftly, with her other hand holding the milk carton, she caught him under his chin, forced his head back. And poured chocolate milk down his face and into his open mouth. Rivulets of chocolate milk ran down his cheeks and neck and down under his sweater.

Perfect. It happened so fast. She was done and out of there, dumping the empty milk container on her way out. Sliding paper plates, napkins, and forks off her tray into the wastebasket; throwing the tray on a stack of them. People didn't know she'd done anything until she was out of there and racing down the hall. She could hear the noise erupt. She expected Grady to come up behind her and knock her down. She guessed she'd have to take it.

Clenching her fists, she tried to brace herself as she went to her locker to get her books. She intended to cut school the rest of the day.

Nothing came about the way she thought it would; Grady didn't come after her. What happened was Miss Denise. She was the seventh-grade class aide.

"Young lady, girl, commere." She came up the hall toward Buhlaire. Probably she was in the lunchroom when Buhlaire took care of Grady.

Miss Denise wasn't as old as Buhlaire's own mom. *Not even a flyspeck as smart*. Buhlaire could do one of two things. She could slam her locker door and ignore Miss Denise, pretend she hadn't heard her. Or she could act nice and respectful. She wanted to tell Miss Denise something smart. Like, "*I know who you are, I just don't know who you think you are.*" Said in her mom's best put-down tone of voice, too. But she was shaking inside.

She closed her locker and didn't say a word. Walked over to Miss Denise, not too slow, not too fast. She stood at just about half-attention. In Plain

City Middle you learned early how much attention was being "cute."

Miss Denise wouldn't take any "stuff from nobody, 'specially you kids."

"You got yourself into something this time," she said to Buhlaire, not unkindly. "Humph. Was it worth it? Get in trouble over Grady? You let him make you mad, you the one pays."

Buhlaire felt as if she might cry. She managed a weak, shaky grin.

"You got even, though," Miss Denise said, and grinned back. Then she said, "Come on, girl. Pay the consequences. If I can, I'll help you out."

She took Buhlaire to the principal's office. Mr. Earl Brown. He came in after she and Miss Denise had been there a few minutes. Buhlaire was sitting in the chair before his desk. He went around her, looking from Miss Denise to her. Miss Denise stood respectfully.

"All right, what is it?" he said as he sat down.

"Little problem with Grady Terrell in the lunchroom." Miss Denise spoke like a lady. "He's still calling her names. Buhlaire decides to do something about it. Poured her chocolate milk down his face."

Stifling what sounded to Buhlaire like a giggle, Miss Denise coughed. Mr. Brown looked as if he were going to grin, but he didn't.

Mr. Earl Brown knew all about her. Always had. *Oh, I wish, I wish!*

"All right, Miss Williams, you can go now."

"Yes, sir."

"Thank you," he said as Miss Denise left them alone.

When the door closed behind her, he said, "Well!" and leaned back.

They were quiet, thinking and glancing at one another. *Everything's okay now*. Mr. Earl Brown was her favorite. She was sure he liked her a lot, too. Like she was his child. She'd made up her mind a long time ago that he belonged to her. When she was in the fifth grade, she had wished he was her dad. She saw him pick up Sandy after school. She told people he was her father, too. It was a joke at first, but then, she believed it. Gossip started, and he had to call her mom, and they'd both talked to Buhlaire. That was the last time she'd thought seriously about having him be her father.

Now, it was like a game. She kidded him — "Your daughter's all grown up!" she said softly, by way of greeting.

"Buhlaire, how're you doing?" Now he said to her, "They tell me your grades are slipping. That's not like you. Things kind of tough for you over at the Water Houses?"

She'd wanted to answer, to smile and shrug, maybe. But what happened was, her shoulders shook, and her eyes filled with tears.

"Ah, Buhlaire, I'm so sorry," he said. He took a box of tissues and handed it to her. She took some, handed it back. She wiped her eyes and blew her nose.

"Take your time," he said as she collected herself. It took awhile.

"Look, let's talk it straight. We've talked since you were in grade school. The problems you had then are the same ones you have now. Forget about Grady a minute. I'm talking about you and your mom and all the Water House people. Do you mind them? Do you mind how you all are?" he asked. He was being careful of the words he used. She knew that, and inside she thanked him for it.

"I guess we look different," she said, finally.

"Not how you look, that isn't it, Buhlaire."

"It's not? I thought it was how I look."

He smiled. "I told you before, it isn't that. You don't really believe me, do you?" He didn't wait for her to answer. "Naturally, you would think it's how you look. A lot of people look like you. I mean mixed enough so that they look fairly white. That's what you're talking about, isn't it? Look around. You aren't the only one."

"I'm not?"

"No, Buhlaire, you're not. You're just self-conscious about yourself. Don't listen to what people say, all that 'outside' stuff."

"That don't bother me," she said. But it did. Being more than one kind made her feel as though she were in a world by herself.

"Well, I'm glad you don't let people bother you."

"It's just — my mom!"

"What about your mom?"

She sighed. Looked away, embarrassed.

After an awkward pause, he said, "Your mom does what she does. She's smart. She's independent. Bluezy Sims does what she does, very well."

Buhlaire didn't dare look at him.

"I mean, she's a fine singer," he added. He stopped there, didn't mention the rest. She didn't dare say anything. But that was it. The rest was why people thought she and her mom really were so different.

The reason was left unspoken between her and Mr. Earl. She liked to call him that: Mister, and then Earl. Yet, it was as if the reason were spoken. Buhlaire went on as if it had been.

"That's one more way they don't like us," she told him. "I mean, all the moms that don't want their kids around me."

"Maybe that's some of it," he said. "You and your mom living on the river with all your Sims in-laws — this is a small town, really. People like to put everybody neatly in place. They go to work, go to school, go to church. They go to the mall, to the movies. Go to basketball games. Everything familiar and in its place. Anybody doesn't want to do what they do, does something different or acts different or even looks different, they're going to talk about them. Maybe even shun them."

"At least, talk about them," she said. "Everybody talks. This town is vicious."

"You sound so old, Buhlaire."

"Well, people think kids don't know. I could tell you things I bet you don't know."

"I bet you could."

"I'm not a snitch," she said. "But I been to some high school parties."

He raised his eyebrows at her. "Has Sandy, my daughter . . ."

"I am not a snitch!" she said again. "Kids run in and run out. The parties are dark. High school kids get *busy*! Time they notice us, we've seen everything and are outta there."

"I see," he said. "But I want you to stay away from high school parties, you hear? Things are going on these days. Sandy better stay away, too."

"I didn't say she went anywhere near high school parties! Mr. Earl, don't you tell her I said she did."

"Buhlaire, I just don't want you to try and grow up too fast. You've got a head on your shoulders, and you have plenty of time."

"But you're not my dad," she teased him, laughing. "I finally found that out. So you can't tell me."

"No, I'm not your dad," he said, smiling.

"My dad was missing. That was in Nam," she said proudly.

She looked up to see him staring at her.

She got serious right away; knew she shouldn't be smiling about that. "I mean, of course, he's not living now. I mean, that was a long time ago, too."

Earl Brown was staring at her in disbelief.

"It's true," she said. "Missing means they finally decided he probably died there in Nam, my dad did. Since they haven't ever found him."

"Where did you get an idea like that?" Mr. Earl

asked. Then he looked sorry he'd spoken. He looked grim.

"Well . . . I guess. I mean," she began, "I don't remember for sure. Seems I always knew." *Probably was Aunt Digna told me. Must've been.* "I mean, after my mom and dad divorced me. My dad first was missing and then was dead in Nam, is what happened."

Principal Earl Brown was very still, there, behind his desk. He was holding a pencil, staring down at his hands. He wrote something on a blank pad. He glanced up at Buhlaire and down again.

"I pride myself on being straight with you young people," he told her. "I've known you a long time. Look, do you know when the Vietnam War ended?"

She shook her head.

"It ended in 1975," he said. He wrote something else on the pad; then he looked up at her. "Maybe it's not my place . . . but it is, it has to be. A principal knows his students. And inside this school, I will call it when I need to. I will make the judgment."

She knew what he meant, kind of. She kept quiet and respectful.

"Buhlaire, I've thought of you just the way I think of Sandy."

She gave him a glistening grin. "You thought of me like your own daughter." *You cared about me. Watched out for me.*

"That's right," he said. "I tell Sandy the truth the best I can, even when I know it might hurt her. I know the truth will set you free." He smiled, tapped his pencil on the pad. "I'm not the first to say that. But, remember, Buhlaire, I said that." He wrote something else. Next, he stopped writing and tore the sheet off. He folded it in half and handed it to her. "Read it when you have a minute by yourself."

She smiled at him. "Mr. Earl, I can read it anytime." She laughed.

He got up then, pushed back his chair. He said he would see Grady next and figure out what to do about him, and her. "You mustn't pour milk on people, Buhlaire." Then he wanted her to know that she was all right. It was all right to be yourself. "Stay yourself, Buhlaire. Part of everything is that you are growing up. Know what happens when you start to grow up?"

"You feel sad?" she asked.

He looked on her kindly. "Sometimes you do," he said. "But I meant, when you start growing up, things don't look the same each day."

"It's like that!" she said. "It's like, I wake up now, and I see things that were always there, only, I see them more, or something."

"You just keep on looking, Buhlaire. And come to see me sometime. Any time you want to talk to somebody, you hear? I'm always around. Even when I have to give detentions."

"Thanks, Mr. Earl." *He likes me; he's my friend.*

"Oh, and Buhlaire. After you read the note, you go on," he said. "I can't say any more about it."

* * *

She went back to her class, already in progress. Kids looked up when she went in. It was a TAG period that lasted over two hours, all afternoon, practically. Talented and Gifted. Kids came from all over Plain City. Rural kids from the countryside around them, rich kids from Uptown. And even her, Buhlaire, from the Water Houses. She'd not really thought about it before now. Yesterday, it was just TAG, something she went to. But today it felt different. It was — she was — Talented and Gifted.

Her spirits stayed up all afternoon. They had journals. You walked into class, and you knew to open your journal to where you'd left off. You wrote about what you were reading. Buhlaire was reading independently. Willy Loman. She smiled. *I mean, reading* Death of a Salesman. *You wouldn't think it was a play you'd like.* Yesterday, she had written that in her journal. Now she wrote about her favorite part. It was a wonder to her how she could walk into a class, just sit down, and begin writing about what she didn't know was on her mind. *"It's the part where his wife tells what Willy, the salesman, is. She says, 'I don't say he is a great man. Willy Loman never made a lot of money. . . . He's not the finest character that ever lived. But he's a human being, and a terrible thing is happening to him. So attention must be paid.' I like that! Then she goes, 'He's not to be allowed to fall into his grave like an old dog. Attention, attention must be finally paid to such a person.' "*

Linda, Willy's wife, felt exactly the same about certain things as Buhlaire.

Buhlaire wrote, "*It means you have to make yourself care for someone, sometimes — is that it? I think about my dad now, and I never did before. I think about Linda, and she is telling me — something. I don't know all the words yet, but I know she's talking so I will understand. Just like Mr. Earl Brown was talking to me so I'd understand, and I don't understand all of it. I feel Linda is kind, kinder than Willy. Mr. Earl is kind.*"

She had his note clutched in her left hand. *The principal, writing me a note!* She looked around, made sure no kids noticed she had something. She held it on her journal page. Smoothed it out. She read it.

Her heart beat hard. A moment, it felt like she couldn't get her breath. She thought she was going to die. She forced herself back to life. The note said: "*Buhlaire. The Vietnam War ended in 1975. You were born around 1980. Think about it. Your dad is, as you know, Theodore 'Junior' Sims. But he never died. He is very much alive and back in this town.*"

3

The Water Houses, Montgomery Falls River

She wasn't positive about what was going on. She thought she must've hollered out. She made sobbing sounds and couldn't help it, although she tried. She didn't care to look around; she knew other students were watching her. Her eyes filled up a minute, but the tears didn't spill. Not long, and the tears went back in somewhere, like something inside soaked them all up. She closed her journal on the note.

Mr. Glenn Daniels, the TAG teacher, stared at her a minute, saying, "Buhlaire? Are you all right? You can be excused; I'll get the aide."

She didn't argue. She never did look up from her desk — couldn't stop her throat from moving, from feeling like it was full. Like she couldn't swallow but she had to keep trying. It was such a shock. It scared her but made her happy. Her dad, alive!

Then, for a long time she was closed in somewhere. She felt she'd fallen far down inside herself. And Mr. Glenn, sending her out with Miss Denise.

"You want to go to the nurse's station? Buhlaire?" Miss Denise talking to her, had her arm around her down the hallway.

"I want to go home," Buhlaire whimpered, sounding like a child.

Something her mom said about children came to her, clear as cold water. *She goes, "Children are mutants. You don't remember childhood, Buhlaire, 'cause young people are all-time mutating to the next stage of young'un. You can't remember from one day to the next because your brain is in a state of flux. Flux? It's change. You are a mutant child, baby, here today and all fluxed tomorrow — heh, heh."*

Remember her telling me that.

Miss Denise saying, "You can't go home unless you have a fever. Are you sick, Buhlaire? Tell the truth, now."

Buhlaire closed her mouth tight. She wouldn't lie.

Miss Denise let her go to the teachers' lounge to lie down until the TAG period was done and she could begin Detention. Time, with her eyes closed, resting quiet, when Miss Denise came to tell her, "Okay, then, Detention starts now."

Not now, not yet, please. "I have to walk around," she managed to say, sitting up.

"No, ma'am," said Miss Denise. "Don't worry, I'll put you in another place from Grady. You each get an hour after every school day for a week. Starting today. Grady, for teasing you. And you for your little show in the lunchroom. And then maybe the two of you will meet with Mr. Brown, speak about it. Won't that be good?"

"No!" Buhlaire said, panic in her eyes. She felt

bad about what she'd done. Couldn't talk about it to Mr. Earl with Grady right there.

"Don't get so upset, Buhlaire. You'll do whatever Mr. Brown wants, okay? That's the way it has to be."

"It wasn't my fault!" Too much was happening all at once.

"Doesn't matter," said Miss Denise. "Any time you play somebody else's dumb game, you're going to lose. Don't let somebody fool you into doing something that'll get yourself in trouble. I know spilling your milk over somebody isn't like you at all, now is it?"

How do you know what I'm like, when I don't even know?

But it was true. She was bewildered by what she'd done. She'd never gone after a kid before, especially a boy.

"No. No, it wasn't like me," Buhlaire said, almost in a whisper. Miss Denise smiled at her. She's not so bad, Miss Denise, she thought.

They went to one of the empty classrooms. Students were already there. Buhlaire was ashamed to be with these few "bad" kids and to be held in after school. That's the way she'd thought about Detention before today. It was for kids you'd expect to break the rules.

She felt she might burst into tears if somebody stared at her hard. Her dad, not dead, and nobody ever telling he was alive made her just sad. Just hurt her so bad inside. Bad kids did stare, but she managed not to cry like a baby. Her mouth turned down. Something hurt her. Maybe in her stomach. Something lay there twisted up and painful, way down inside.

Students weren't allowed to talk during Detention or read anything that didn't have to do with school. They had to sit up and not sleep on their arms. Buhlaire didn't feel like reading. So she let her thoughts come as they pleased. Sat there, straight and tall.

Miss Denise was in the room, grading papers and writing in the grade book. In the first few minutes she'd asked Buhlaire, "You want to help me with these papers? You read off the grade, and I'll write it in the book. Huh? Want to? But you don't have to — just something for you to do."

She said no to Miss Denise, she wouldn't help grade papers. She just wanted to do her time of Detention. It might've been something, though, to see the grades everybody else was getting. But she really didn't care. She did well, herself, because she liked what she was doing and didn't care about doing better than somebody else.

Bad kids eyed her. Snickered. It dawned on her that she was different from them, and not because of herself.

They're different, too. I never knew that before.

They were always the ones — the bad kids. They didn't count. She looked around at them when they weren't looking at her. Looked at them as though for the first time. *Maybe they aren't even so bad. Maybe they feel bad about their own selves the way I do. Huh. She knew their names. Tommy Dansforth. Nathaniel Towne. And Becky Burdan. They aren't even a "they." They're even different from one another.* She had never talked to any of them. She never talked to most kids in school. Just ones in Chorus with her.

So you can't class these kids and me all as one. Huh. Thinking that, she found Aunt Digna close in her mind. Saw her at the big window, watching for her. Aunt Digna wouldn't even wonder where she was just yet. *Probably thinks I'm doing what I always do. Walking out in the snow.* Unless Mr. Earl called to tell her otherwise, which Buhlaire felt sure he wouldn't.

He's my friend, Mr. Earl. He told me about my dad when nobody else ever did. How is it my dad's alive? All at once, Buhlaire started to tremble; her mouth was so dry, she could hardly swallow. There was an ache over one eye.

She really did feel like putting her head down. *Miss Denise, I'm sick. No, you're not! You just need to sit still awhile and calm down. Aunt Digna is all-time telling me: "Calm down, Buhlaire, life be the same road whether you run or walk it."*

Yeah? Yesterday, my dad was dead. Today, he's alive! 1975, 1980! I wasn't even born if he died in '75. I am so stupid. Didn't even think! That's what Sandy was trying to tell me, saying it doesn't figure.

Trying hard to calm herself, Buhlaire stretched her legs out under the desk. She found she was clutching her hands together. Now she rubbed them and let them lie side by side, palms down on the desktop. She took a deep breath. She made a pyramid with her hands, stared at them. Long fingers.

Thinking about her mom. Bluezy Sims wasn't in town at Delmore's in Plain City every weekend. Bluezy might be anywhere in a three- to four-hundred-mile circle around Plain City. As far north as Cleveland singing in a club, or De-troit, and south to Lexington or Louisville and even Memphis. She'd come home and fall into bed, dead tired from the road after a long gig. Buhlaire might not even know she was there. Bluezy could do that to her.

Then, I hear a cough in the next room. Remember, Mom is home; so I want to see her. Run in, "Mom! Hey! Come sing with me at the piano." She twitches awake. And barely opens an eye. She goes, "Girl, you have no sense, waking somebody hasn't got any sleep, working all hours, too." Hoarse voice, croaking. "Barely can talk as it is. Girl, give me some space. But first, give me a li'l kiss and a hug."

Oh, Mom! Buhlaire thought now. And down deep and quiet, there waited a strong suspicion. That Bluezy and even Bluezy's sister Babe — even all her dad's family: Aunt Sydney, Uncle Sam, Aunt Digna, Uncle Buford, and others — all of them had let her down. *Even the little kids. Some of them are my relatives, too. Everybody probably knowing everything. But me, I, not knowing. My own dad! Where has he been?*

Not long, it seemed, and this Detention hour was over. Four-fifteen, late. All of them with Detention unwound themselves and tramped down the hall out of school. Seeming ashamed of themselves or one another, they didn't glance around. They didn't talk, or say good-bye.

Outside and cold. The sun looked ready to disappear behind low clouds. Unseen, it would soon go down.

Better to go home this first Detention day, Buhlaire thought, and see if Mr. Earl has told Aunt Digna anything. She'll be watching for me.

She took long strides through the cold. Being Buhlaire, bareheaded. How I look? she wondered. *Well, stand up tall, anyhow.* And so she did.

Boy, Grady better not be following me now. Better not come near me.

Suddenly, she slowed down. *Maybe he's going to push me. Go biking out there at the edge of town, and he tries hitting me hard. For what I did to him? He knows it's his fault I did it. All a-time teasing, signifying at me. He won't do anything. 'Cause he likes me. Least, he did. Anyhow, I'm not going out there, with the Detention. Hate that word.*

She kept her eyes on a space on the sidewalk ahead of her moving feet. Going down from the Midway district in the opposite way from striding out of town. She was edging along the lowland, skirting the slowly rising landmass to her back that finally shaped Midway and Uptown. The Montgomery Falls River outlined the base of the landmass at its bottom land.

Slowly, sounds of the city quieted down, and the

rhythms of country and Montgomery Falls iced-over River filled the crisp air. Almost before she knew it, Buhlaire was on familiar territory. She stepped on the first, planked walkway. She had walked so fast, over a mile, her bookbag slung over one shoulder. Striding, it took her no more than fifteen minutes to come in sight of the sycamore trees. Home land. Home ground. The Water Houses, where she came from. *I'm the Water House child.*

The sounds of home ground, or anything about the Water Houses, wasn't easy for Buhlaire to know clearly. She had feelings about the place, too, mixed in with sights and sounds. It all had to do with the light and shade. And with going, of light fading to dark. Buhlaire didn't know where the light was, she was so often in the dimness.

Outside the stands of sycamores, there was little sign at all that houses were there. The surrounding, bare winter trees made deep shadows, blending, softening into the landscape. With a half foot of snow and the cold like something living on its own, the trees were awash in dreary, foggy shade. Amidst the trees and shade, the Water Houses were invisible.

The smell of moss, even a scent of river water turned to ice, stayed with Buhlaire. River water ran smoothly, she knew, way deep down where the fishes went to wait out the cold. She paused to stand still in the sycamore woods covering this bottom land of the river. She let the bookbag slip down to her wrist; strap in her hand, she rested the bag on the icy snow now crusting on top as the temperature dropped. *See my breath, looking all cold and white in the air. Breath is warm, though, coming out.*

Water Houses were unlike water and more like tree houses. Better to call them stilt houses, she was thinking. She stopped a moment at this spot to look at everything and breathe it in. The sight of it filled her up with mixed feelings, light and dark.

The houses, six of them, sat eight feet off the ground on concrete poles that were reinforced with metal bars inside. The poles went down deep into the ground and were sunk in concrete blocks.

Mom goes, "We haven't lost any Water Houses yet. And we won't. Oh, maybe a few of the supports, but no houses. Not the way we reconstructed."

People said spring rains could cause the river to overflow. In Buhlaire's mind, she could hear Aunt Babe just as clear, saying about it: "*Montgomery Falls swelled up one time . . . all of a sudden flashed a flood. The way it come all at once in front of our eyes — mercy! Before me and your aunt Digna even notice it rising swift, it's upon you . . . here today, and gone tomorrow. A mystery of God.*"

Folks said that once in a great while came a long, cool flooding that lasted. Buhlaire hadn't seen it, but she'd heard that in some springtimes, the Montgomery Falls River could become a whole flood plain, hundreds of feet wide and a couple of feet deep, maybe even deeper than that. Deep water flood, as far as she could see, maybe, trying to reach far up into town but not quite able to. Wanting to flood every Water House, if it could, if it could reach up that high. It hadn't flooded like that in a long kinda time, Aunt Digna had said. But maybe Buhlaire would see something like that in her life.

The Water Houses were two-story buildings, each one with apartments that her mom rented out. On the outside, they looked something like army barracks. They were made of wood that never got painted. To the unpracticed eye, they looked old and battered. More than likely, people thought Buhlaire's family was poor, having to live in shabby houses down by the river. Digna called the wood redwood, but Buhlaire couldn't see it. The wood was silver-gray, and dark in places where water seeped into the boards. Aunt Digna said over the years the plain old boards had been replaced with the redwood by Uncle Buford and his crew. Some of his men were also related to Buhlaire. *Aunt Digna goes, " 'You don't paint redwood,' Bluezy says. Shoot. You could stain it redwood, though, and make it look halfway decent. 'Give that redwood a couple of coats so it looks like it's worth something,' is what I tell her. But she don't listen to nobody."*

Buhlaire knew her mom did lots of fixing up of the Water Houses. Both Uncle Buford and Uncle Sam worked on the premises as well as in other places around Plain City. They made all kinds of wood stuff for the houses. And all of the walkways up to the private boundary of their property were made of planks hewn by Uncle Buford's crew.

Bluezy didn't like people knowing her business, but anybody on the river all of the time knew that reconstruction against flooding went on inside the houses. Treated-wood floors, reinforced cement walls, storm doors. That's all Buhlaire knew about. Her mom kept very good care of her property. Had it posted, too — Private Property and No Trespassing signs in loud red and black. But that didn't mean anything. Other people who didn't live in the houses wandered along the river in summer, or tramped around in all seasons. Sometimes they walked up to the Water Houses, right up to a renter's door, looking in windows, as though Buhlaire's home ground didn't belong to anybody.

Buhlaire was seeing the whole home place before her — land, river, and Water Houses. She was thinking, *I'll go ask Uncle Sam about his brother, my dad.* Sam and Buford and her dad, and Digna and Sydney, were all brothers and sisters.

She slipped behind the houses, keeping low and hoping Aunt Digna didn't catch a glimpse of her. Aunt Digna might think she needed to come along, if she guessed where Buhlaire was going.

"Don't think about it and get scared," she told herself. "Just do it. Just walk on over and do it." She steeled herself inside. *He's your uncle Sam. Never talks much, none of them do. Once in a while, we go out with him. But he has never been tough with me.*

We all live down here, and people get confused about us. Mom's sister-in-law, Aunt Digna, lives with me and Mom. Mom's sister, Aunt Babe Strickland, lives next door to us. People think it's strange, I guess. But Aunt Babe likes being by herself a lot. Doesn't want to be too dependent on Aunt Digna or Mom. And, since Mom's away a lot, Aunt Digna gets to watch over me — too much, if you ask me. We don't really all live together, I mean tight and close. When Mom's here, it's like we all get along with her, talking to her. She talks to everybody else. It's like we are pieces on a chain, not even touching. Mom is the chain's big center piece of gold.

"Okay. Okay. Keep going," Buhlaire told herself.

She looked in the workshop behind Uncle Sam's, but only Uncle Buford was there with two of his crew. One of them had light-colored hair in waves down his back. Uncle Sam's hair was dark. Buhlaire wondered all of a sudden if her dad had the same dark hair.

"Hey-hey," she said, looking in on them. Uncle Buford didn't turn around. The other two looked over at him. She didn't want to ask Uncle Buford anything with them there.

"Hey, Buhlaire-Marie," said Uncle Buford.

Nobody ever called her that but Uncle Sam and Uncle Buford. So stiff — polite. "You seen Uncle Sam?" she asked.

"Seen him on the river," said Uncle Buford. "Got in his mind to find some fish, but I don't think so."

"Huh," she said. "Like to see that."

He turned around then. She saw his steely eyes. She shrunk back just a little. But his voice was the same, neutral, when he spoke again. "Mother's back in town."

That made Buhlaire hold still inside.

"Not here, yet, but around," he said. "Talk to Sam." He turned again to his power tools.

The guy with long hair sang out, "Bluezy's back in town!" He grinned at Buhlaire.

"Hey," she said. He nodded in return. *I know you. Seen you all the time.* It was so funny how she felt she was noticing for the first time what she'd always known was there. Her relatives. *Like my eyes are open, but I been asleep.* But her mom. "*Mother's back in town.*" How come everybody knew something before she did? At least Uncle Buford let her know. *Wonder if Aunt Digna knows, too?*

She hurried over to the river, forgetting to worry about Digna seeing her. Forgetting Bluezy for the moment, so used to being without her. She walked by Uncle Sam's house, where Aunt Sydney, the other Sims sister, leaned out the door looking at the children she baby-sat. They peeked around Aunt Sydney.

"Hey, Aunt Sydney," Buhlaire called, as sweetly as she knew how. "You'll catch your cold." But she didn't slow down. Aunt Sydney nodded. Buhlaire called to the children. "Hey, Buddy, little Dale, Carleen Dee." When the children tried to squeeze past Aunt Sydney to run after Buhlaire, Aunt Sydney forced them back. Said something to them. One of them wailed.

Buhlaire walked along the bank of the shore. Drifting snow came almost to her knees, and she had to lift her legs to get through it. She didn't see

Uncle Sam. She turned away from the shore and stepped in a long stride down and out onto the river's solid ice. She could call out for Uncle Sam, and that way, when he answered back, she'd follow the sound of his voice.

The river took some twists and turns here. Trees were thicker all the way along. Minutes passed as she walked among them. They rose and then hung out over the river. *Snap!* But awesome. It made looking downstream bring a feeling to Buhlaire as if she were in church, in a cathedral. A sacred, praying place. She sighed deeply and took a long breath. Cold air filled her lungs. It felt good, too, she thought.

She watched her shins go in the snow and disappear. She looked behind her to see the kind of trail she made.

All in the open. That quick. Like a nightmare, she saw bad news coming out of nowhere. Creeping up on her. It looked like a bear, but it was human.

His voice slithered at her, suddenly, scaring her, saying, "Evening, honey." His bare hands dangled at his sides. They looked gray, ashy with the cold. The stranger smiled at her.

What's he doing down here? She didn't know him, never seen him. His clothes were shaggy and many-layered. She could see the grime caked around the collars and cuffs of them. "There's a kitchen at the shelter in town," she said, turning to face him and backing away. Her voice sounded shaky.

She knew shelter people mostly as folks down on

their luck. They didn't want to hurt anybody, or look for trouble. Whoever this was, she thought, could be the bad-luck-for-you Aunt Digna was always telling her she'd run into out in the countryside. *Some piece of trash, blown in off the interstate.*

Buhlaire put her hand inside her suit, like somebody would do on television. She imagined a weapon there. She closed her hand as if she were closing it around something deadly with a handle. She fingered the imaginary trigger, still backing away from him and never taking her eyes off him. She had a searing thought: *Maybe he's my dad? No, it can't be.* There was no time to think more. The man was smiling at her, casually coming toward her.

"Honey, you know there's nothing inside that suit but pretty you. Out here all by your lonesome?"

He can't see the houses for the trees. "Mister, I'm — not — " She didn't finish.

Swiftly, the stranger moved toward her. Panicked, afraid to turn away, Buhlaire backpedaled in the deep snow. She yelled, "Uncle Sam! *It's Buhlaire! Uncle Sam, help me!*" There was a fearful urgency to her voice.

The man's feet crunched through the snow. Looking all around, not knowing whether Buhlaire was fake-yelling, he moved warily.

She was away from him, but not far enough. She knew never to trust strangers. For the first time in her life, she felt she might really be in trouble.

Something was at the edge of her sight, in the

trees on the shore, and moving like a swift animal. She took a second to see and never knew anything that big could move so fast.

"Well, then, Buhlaire-Marie." It was Uncle Sam, breaking through the trees, all six foot six inches of power-him.

The stranger froze in his tracks, looking.

"Uncle Sam!" *Oh, my uncle Sam!*

Uncle Samson Leroy Sims was at the shore. He had his ice hatchet in one hand, poised in a throw position higher than his right shoulder. In his left hand he held a short line of small fish. He was bigger than life, bigger than the whole outdoors to Buhlaire.

"Uncle Sam, I came looking for you!"

"And found me, too," he said. He wasn't smiling as he hooked the fish to a clip on his belt. He never took his eyes off the man in Buhlaire's path.

"Now, I don't mean no trouble," the bad-news stranger thought to say in a hurry. "Just passing through." He tried grinning, but Uncle Sam wasn't making friends.

"If I were you," Uncle Sam said, "I'd pass through someplace else. This property is posted private. And if I were you, I'd pass on out of town forever."

The stranger raised his hands, yielding in this gesture of surrender. "I'm real cold," he said. "She says there's a shelter in town."

"No, sir," Uncle Sam said. "Buhlaire-Marie, you come walk over here."

Quickly, Buhlaire was off the ice and over to Uncle Sam. He put his hand lightly on her shoulder and kept her to his side, away from the raised hatchet.

"And you, mister, go. Now. Use the river, keep going on out of town where you can hear that interstate," Uncle Sam said. "And when you come to it, find a way on it. When I get home, I'll give the local talent a call. They'll see you find some place away is warm. You can't miss 'em, either. They're the ones who drive the white cars with the silver-and-blue medallion. Says, Plain City *Po*-lice."

4

Aunt Digna, Aunt Babe

It's too bad on the stranger, thought Buhlaire. *Uncle Sam was mean. Maybe the man would've hurt me. Maybe not.*

When she said that to Uncle Sam, he told her, "Buhlaire-Marie, there are times when you can take no chances. You have to do the safe thing. And the safe thing was to scare the man off."

They trudged along the trail they all knew so well along the shore, through the sycamores. "He said he was hungry and cold," Buhlaire said. "Maybe he'll freeze himself to death out here." *My dad's not cold. Not anymore.*

"Huh," was all Uncle Sam said.

"Don't you care about that stranger?" Buhlaire asked.

"No," he said, "I do not. I won't waste my sympathy." He had his hand on her shoulder as though to guide her.

She found it nice to be next to Uncle Sam and close. *Like walking beside a giant friend.* She knew to stay quiet, to make the closeness last. But being so near such a strong man made her feel good, and made her want to talk.

"Care for your fellow man," she'd read somewhere. Maybe it was in her history book. Or maybe her literature language arts text. It could be from a poem — "Care for your fellow" — she was eager to talk about it.

"Care for your fellow, sister, human beings," she said to her uncle Sam.

"Huh," Uncle Sam said, like he didn't think much of the idea.

"But if that had-a been my dad come out of nowhere — " she began. It was easier than she had thought. She held her breath and said the rest. "We'd-a helped him, given him food if he needed it." *Wouldn't we? Go 'head, lie and tell me he's dead. Just tell me he's here, and I can find him.*

She drew in her shoulders, didn't dare look at Uncle Sam. She let her breath out quietly as her heart raced. *Oh, please, tell me about my dad.*

He took his hand off her shoulder. She almost didn't feel it. The light touch going, nearly taking the memory of it away, as though it had never been. He stepped in front of her to lead her home. And she stopped a moment, letting the hurt wash down clear into her toes and out the soles of her boots into the frozen earth. Like lightning being grounded.

They all of them are just so hard when they want to be. When it comes to my own sweet dad.

The Water Houses came in sight through the

trees. One minute they were nowhere; the next, they were there. Buhlaire stood in between houses, not going, not looking at anything. Until Uncle Sam thought to turn to her and say, "We'll go in tonight. Early set. I told Digna we'd have to take you. Be ready. I know it's a school night. But Bluezy said to bring you for an hour. So."

The whole time he spoke, she stood at attention. The white jumpsuit gathered in the last sun left on the day. She looked like a white streak, a loud exclamation in the muted light.

Buhlaire nodded at Uncle Sam, looking just to the side of him. *Everybody always does what Mom says.* Good, she thought. At least her mom wanted to see her. "All right," she told him. "I'll be ready."

Once the danger had passed, Uncle Sam's friendliness was over. Maybe some caring for Bluezy and Digna had caused him to come to Buhlaire's rescue. *He'd probably do that for anybody.* And now there was the duty that allowed him to give her over to Bluezy.

She was used to it. It was all right. She would get to see her mom, and that was something. But the hurt place inside her kept her dad in a mist, in a drifting fog that was never ending.

Now. See what Aunt Digna's up to. She went through the trees from Uncle Sam's. Suddenly she noticed that the whole day was going. Winter light was like lamp light being lowered. By the time she was home, it was eveningtime, a quiet dusk marching along the land. The night held back in stillness and in dark just beyond the river. Aunt Digna had already turned on the table lamp at the window.

Digna Sims was in her evening chair, looking out. Aunt Babe Strickland, Bluezy's sister, who never married, was there, too, but out of view. Digna and Babe were so different. Babe didn't like the curtains open when it got dark. Digna liked to watch the night coming on.

I told Aunt Digna once, "But when it's dark, you can't see what might be looking in." And she goes, "Who so ever stops and looks in, sees me, and they had better look out."

Buhlaire came inside. She adjusted to the sudden light and let her bookbag fall to her feet. Now she could feel the soreness in her shoulder where the bag strap had cut into her for so long. There was a square of extra carpeting inside the door where she was standing. She took up a whisk broom, brushing the snow off her pant legs and boots onto the carpet square.

"Hey, you all," she said. She finished with the broom and stepped in off the carpet.

"Can't say a proper hello?" asked Aunt Babe. Her voice was wispy and thin, like high wind through old, spindly trees.

"Aunt Babe, hullo. How you doing today?"

Aunt Babe looked, but she could see only shapes coming and going. Sometimes, they moved into her view too quickly, frightening her. Buhlaire was always careful to move slowly toward her. Babe lived in a world of shadows in the small apartment next to Buhlaire and Digna's home. Uncle Buford had cut open a wall to make a door through to her place.

Aunt Digna goes, "Easier for me to care for her, watch her, with that door. And she can find her way in here when she chooses to."

Babe's blue-filmed eyes searched for Buhlaire; fixed on Buhlaire as she came slowly toward her aunt. She gave Aunt Babe a peck on her cheek.

Warm. So soft. Aunt Babe reached for Buhlaire's hair, held it close to her eyes. "Color of straw and gold, mixed, I remember," she said. "Is it, still?"

"Shoot, I guess. Getting darker, though," Buhlaire said. She kneeled and shut her eyes.

Aunt Babe had Buhlaire's head in her hands. She closed her fingers, shaping them into a ball over a bunch of Rasta twists. "You smell like the river," Aunt Babe murmured, twisting and stroking the full, springy softness of Buhlaire's curlings. She chuckled. "You brought that river right inside this house — is the water rising?" Babe asked. "It sits inside my head, a long water, coming."

"Aunt Babe, it's winter," Buhlaire said. "The river's frozen deep."

"Ah, I forget, sometimes. Winter. Yes, now I feel the house heat. Gas bottled heat. If I had my way, there'd be iron stoves in every room."

Aunt Digna cleared her throat. By that, she meant to change the subject. She had her arms folded across her narrow chest. Of the three women, she was in the middle in age between Babe and Bluezy. Babe was oldest, seemed much older than her years.

Digna never liked talking about what could be but wasn't. She was not so tall and thin as Bluezy, and had none of her liveliness. There were no bright warm flares in Digna's eyes. Something had washed out of her. What was left was worn down, but patient. Stubborn.

"Aunt Digna, hi," Buhlaire said. As always, they reached for each other. Hands. They held hands. "How you doing?" Buhlaire asked. And felt her own heat enter into Aunt Digna's limp fingers. She held on, and finally, Digna gave, and held on, too.

"Doing the best I can," Aunt Digna said. Her aunt liked it when they said the same things to each other every day, Buhlaire could tell. "How you doing, baby?"

"Tired. Been out fishing with Uncle Sam." Not quite the truth. Buhlaire worried about telling what was true. Over in the corner, Aunt Babe's hands fluttered, parting the air in front of her as if to see better. She had heard disquiet in Buhlaire's voice.

"Is something wrong?" Aunt Babe asked. She looked alarmed.

Buhlaire sighed deeply. She never could get by Aunt Babe's sixth sense. So she told about the stranger. When she finished, Aunt Digna let Buhlaire's hands go. She got up to pull the blinds down and close the curtains, something she would hardly ever do.

Digna didn't want to alarm Aunt Babe. But she told Buhlaire, "As long as my brothers and Sydney are here, I'll stay with you and Babe and your mama.

But how come people are walking around all the time, looking at ferns and moss and such? They never seen these tall trees, neither? Nature ain't nothing new. They getting like you, Buhlaire, can't stay put, wandering every which a-way. I keep telling Bluezy, I wouldn't be surprised if they're just looking to steal."

"Your mama, back in town," Aunt Babe told Buhlaire.

"Babe, I'm not finished," Aunt Digna said sharply.

"Well, you should be."

"Hush up! Keep still!" Aunt Digna told her.

"Uncle Sam already spoke to me about Mom," Buhlaire said. *No, it was Uncle Buford first told me. I went to find out about my dad from Uncle Sam.*

They fell silent. Buhlaire waited, she got to her feet to sit down again in the easy chair away from the table. She didn't even look around more than a second. Carpet, table, chairs, not new, not beautiful, faded somewhat. And so much a part of her life, she knew each piece so well, she accepted it and forgot about it as soon as she saw it. But if a piece had been missing, she would have noticed and screamed at them about it. But all was in place. All was home. She could glance at both Aunt Digna and Aunt Babe. They watched her. She wondered how much Aunt Babe could see.

A plump woman was Babe, shrinking back, away from the front window. She had a round face that she powdered every day. She wore no lipstick, and the powder made Aunt Babe seem ghostly. She crocheted through the daylight hours, counting stitches and often asking Digna, "Is it time? Is it time, yet?" Digna would tell her when it was time to change a thread color and what color would go next. Babe could no longer tell the difference.

Aunt Digna kept accounts having to do with the Water Houses. She paid all of the crews, collected all of the rents. By evening, her books were put away. She took them out each Sunday, to be ready for the week. Buhlaire had never looked inside them. *Wonder does she pay Uncle Buford, Uncle Sam? Must. And Mom? Mom tells her who to pay and what. I know she does.*

Aunt Digna said to Buhlaire, "Better clean up now, change that outfit. We are going out."

"Uncle Sam told me we were," Buhlaire said.

"Well, and I have supper almost done. So get going."

"Seems like the night has come down," said Aunt Babe. She put on her head scarf, as she always did when night came. She gathered up her needlework. She seemed to be thinking about going out-of-doors. But only in her mind did she go anywhere, usually.

Aunt Digna goes, "Behind Babe's eyes, there's a country of if-I'd-a-done's and but-I'm-afraid-to's."

I feel for her — good ol' Aunt Babe. Want to always make sure she's safe. "Why don't you come on and go with us tonight, Aunt Babe?" Buhlaire said.

Aunt Babe sucked in her breath. Unseeing eyes, wide, she said, "I might fall."

"I'll hold on to you," Buhlaire said. "I'll help you along through the snow."

"No, no, I don't want to. It's too cold out."

"Oh, come on, Aunt Babe. It'll be fun," Buhlaire urged her. "Come on and go with us."

"Leave her alone. Let her stay home if she's so scared of the cold," Aunt Digna said.

Aunt Babe held her head high. "I don't feel so good this evening. Tell Bluezy I'll see her when she gets home. She can sing to me then."

"Babe." Aunt Digna, changing the subject, said, "You feel like setting the table?"

Without another word, Aunt Babe rose from her chair. In the silence, she felt her way down the wall and opened the door that went through to her home. There was a faint line along the wall where her hand had brushed it so many times.

"Well, I guess she don't feel like it," said Aunt Digna. "She gets mad at me on a dime! You know, sometimes she forgets how it's so cold. And then, when she reminds herself, she acts all funny and out of sorts."

"How can she forget about cold?" Buhlaire asked. "It gets into everything." *My dad won't be cold. He's alive.*

"But we don't know what it's like for her," Aunt Digna said. "She lives in the gray of her eyes."

I thought blindness was black! My dad's not blind.

"Maybe she thinks she's outside under the shade trees. Got summer in her brain. And so she forgets the cold," said Digna.

Buhlaire sat there, taking off her boots, her shoes, then her socks. Her feet were yellow and felt damp from the cold. She didn't know that she would say it, but she did. It came out. She was thinking, yellow feet — and it came out evenly and carefully. Aunt Digna couldn't miss it: "My dad's alive. He is here in this town. Why come nobody told me?"

"You can do it for me, then. Set the table, Buhlaire," Aunt Digna said, just as smoothly. "Take over for Aunt Babe. She's so out of sorts these days. Call her to supper when you finish."

You heard me, you mean old bag.

"You see these walls? The lamp tables?" Digna asked, as if she were talking about water glasses and dishes, setting the table still. "You ever wonder there's not a picture hanging anywhere? Not any bric-a-brac or a knickknack on a table? How come I lock all my drawers?"

Buhlaire had no time to think about that. Going out of the room, Digna was still talking. "Take that first tablecloth on top, top drawer of the breakfront, Buhlaire."

Quickly, Buhlaire did as she was told.

She hurried with the tablecloth, straightening and smoothing it out over the table.

"Get out of that jumpsuit and get bathed," was the next thing Digna told her. "Hurry some, because there's not a lot of time. We don't want to be late."

In the kitchen, Buhlaire took off her jumpsuit and stuffed it in the laundry hamper. She didn't take the time to think about the other — bric-a-brac. But her dad rested there, invisible, in the dark back of her thoughts as night pressed against all the windows.

She went into the bathroom where there were pink plastic curtains over the window, and black night on the windowpanes. Buhlaire pulled down the blind and took her bath. Slowly, her brain emptied, as water, hot as she could stand it, climbed over her.

And on through the evening, small events of this night were full of satisfaction for her. Getting clean. Wrapping the towel around her. Going into her room.

On the other side of the wall was Bluezy's room. Bluezy loved the color she called mauve. Not pink, not strawberry, not raspberry. But mauve, with a silken mauve quilt and pillow shams to match. And mauve curtains, long and draped. With a mauve carpet, even a different shade of it.

Mom *mauve*! thought Buhlaire. Mauver, mother, ha! And she giggled.

She threw off the towel when she saw the box.

"Aunt Digna!" Buhlaire hollered.

Digna called back, "It's something new for you to wear tonight. Bluezy sent it."

"Oh!" Buhlaire tore open the box. "Wow! Cooel!" she shouted. It was an outfit, light blue velvet, a one-piece jumpsuit. "Oh man, I love it!" She didn't realize, at once, that there was a second box under the first. She dressed in the new-smelling, softest velvet. *Oh, how beautiful!*

She looked in the floor-length mirror, turning this

way and that. *Neat!* It was the sleekest outfit she'd ever had. *Mom! Thanks a lot. You are a cool dude, Mom.* It all made her feel good inside.

In the mirror, she saw the second box just sitting there. Never even saw it! Went over. She held her breath and tore it open and pulled out a dressy dark blue velvet coat. She threw it on. It was just so pretty.

"Aunt Digna, commere!"

Digna sauntered in, leaned on the doorjamb. "Well. Miss Blue Lady."

Buhlaire laughed and turned around and around on her tiptoes so Aunt Digna could see the whole thing. "How do you like it?"

"Looking good on you, baby. You look pretty in blue. You need to do something with that head-a-hair, though. Can't you do something?"

"I happen to like it how it is."

"Fine, but when was the last time you had a comb through it?"

"You don't have to comb it. I run my fingers in it and twist it."

"I got some blue velvet ribbon. You want to tie it up?"

"Let me see it."

Digna got the ribbon. It was light blue and a good match. "Did you go buy this for me?" Buhlaire asked her.

"No ma'am. I keep such as that handy for Babe's sewing."

For the next twenty minutes, Buhlaire worked on

her hair and the ribbon. When she was finally satisfied, she had tied it tightly on her head just above her forehead and around in front of her ears. Her curls came down covering them. She worked the curls on each side of her face so they tumbled free over the ribbon.

"There," she said.

When she went back into the living room, the table was set. Aunt Babe was already there.

"Sorry I took so long," Buhlaire said.

"Do you look like a young lady?" Aunt Babe wanted to know.

Aunt Digna brought in the food. "She's in two shades of blue velvet," she told Babe.

Babe smiled, nodded.

The food smelled so good. "Love meatballs and spaghetti!" Buhlaire said.

"It's not my favorite," said Aunt Babe. "I prefer vegetarian."

"Eat just the salad, then," huffed Digna. "This ain't about you."

"Would you like a peanut butter sandwich?" Buhlaire asked. "I can make it for you."

"Toasted, whole wheat. And some raspberry jelly."

"Don't you move," Digna told Buhlaire. "I'll fix it for Miss Queen here, who prefers vegetarian. Peanut butter. Lord."

They ate in silence. Every now and again, Buhlaire would smile happily. Digna would humpf. Buhlaire gave a gentle knee rub to sweet Aunt Babe.

Love you, Aunt Babe. You can always count on me. They were mostly quiet like that, Babe and Buhlaire, as Digna cleared off the table and Buhlaire held Babe's hand. It wasn't that the two of them talked so much to one another. It was that they were close in their minds — feeling, caring for one another without the need for words. They were calm like that in the house. Then Uncle Sam came.

5

Delmore's

You could cut your hand on the creases in Uncle Sam's charcoal-gray trousers, Buhlaire thought. He came to get her and Aunt Digna and take them out. No way did he look like the same Uncle Sam off fishing, who had scared away a menace. *His eyes will still look everywhere but at me.*

He had on a gray overcoat and a dark wool sweater. His starched white shirt collar showed beneath the sweater. He wore black dress shoes and gray dress socks. It looked as if he'd had a haircut since Buhlaire saw him earlier. And he had shaved. She could smell his aftershave.

She and Aunt Digna went with him in his pickup truck. Buhlaire thought it was cool to drive a pickup. In the daylight, you could see it was a gorgeous ruby-red. Now it was night and too dark to see the color.

They were in the truck with the heater on; Buhlaire was cozy. *Aunt Digna goes: "Humph. A velvet jumpsuit is more for pretty-and-show than for warmth. Glad she at least got you a short coat to go with it."* So disapproving of Bluezy's taste. Digna had on a possum-fur coat dyed to look like mink. It was a fine-looking long coat, handed over to her from her sister-in-law. *Poor animals, before they were ever a coat.* Bluezy even had it cut off and fitted to Aunt Digna's shape.

They took the road along the sycamores and left the Water Houses behind. The downtown of Plain City looked dead and dreary as they passed, empty of people, with everything locked up tight. *Empty of her dad?* They took the interstate out of town for a short way, and then onto Hill High Road. They took a careful climb up another hill onto what seemed like a flat, high table of farmland. Everything looked eerie in the full-moon light. Fields of snow shone a bluish shade of dark, looking cold and ghosty.

They went about a mile down the road that crunched with a hardpack melt — snow that thawed thick and slushy in the sunlight but froze again in the subzero nights. The road had been snowplowed and layered. Then it was packed by traffic going to and from a truck plant about five miles on.

The pickup's high beams snagged lone houses here and there, and blundered into a run-down filling station. *Friday the 13th. Screams in the night. Ooooh! Scary, boys and girls!*

The three of them rode in silence. The night-and-fright was made less for Buhlaire with Uncle Sam on one side and Aunt Digna on the other. She could barely see their profiles in the dashboard glow. She watched, fascinated, as the high beams played over the landscape.

"I'm all warm, sitting beside you in that fur coat," Buhlaire thought to say to Aunt Digna. Just then, Delmore's ten-foot blue-and-yellow neon sign rushed at them out of the dark. *Like the sign is loudness, screams, but there's no sound at all.*

"Thank goodness we're here," Aunt Digna said. "I feel like I'm on fire." She might complain, but Buhlaire saw her running her ungloved hand along the plush fur lapels of the coat.

Delmore's — coming at us. Made from our headlights sweeping. That's how it seemed to Buhlaire. *Pickup goes so fast! Straight up, the high beams bring us Delmore's out of nothing and nowhere.* She felt all jumpy with nerves.

On the marquee was the playbill, lit up in white light behind large black letters — "Now Showing: *Bluezy Sims.*"

It gave Buhlaire a thrill to see her mom's name in those black letters.

Usually, her mom picked the time Buhlaire could see her perform — as she had now. "Passed a miracle," was what Aunt Digna called it when her sister-in-law commanded they come out in the dark to see her. Night was the same as day to Bluezy.

The huge Delmore's sign looked to be all there was to the roadhouse. The building was dark, as if it were closed. It was low and long, right by the side of the road. It might've been deserted, except for the cars all parked in rows in the front parking area. The gleaming neon reflected on car roofs, wavering and flowing like a stream of colors. Delmore's had no windows and no doors to mark the front. It had side windows, though, and a door, also on the side. There was a heavy steel back door with an exit sign.

The customer entrance was just around the corner. Uncle Sam held the door for them. Buhlaire wanted to lead the way. It was exciting to be out on a school night in such a place. She had the privilege because her mom worked there. But some of her classmates weren't allowed to go where alcohol was served. Some wouldn't even want to go.

Buhlaire had expected quiet, and few people inside. Yet, she had seen the cars. Not all of it had connected. She brought it together now. Inside, she heard music. Walking down the dim hall, the walls twinkled with tiny star lights. The dark green-and-gold wallpaper made her feel as if she were in Hollywood; it glistened magically when the little lights blinked on-off, on-off. Sound rushed in, bar glasses tinkled, and voices rose and fell. Then came the blare and throb of the jukebox.

Good. We're on time. Bluezy hadn't started her set.

"Welcome to Delmore's, folks. Check your coats?" A counter cut into the wall at the end of the hall. Behind it was the coat-check lady and a walk-in area with coats and jackets on racks. Buhlaire couldn't recall the lady's name. Didn't really recognize her.

" 'Lo, Blanche," Uncle Sam said. She took his coat as he handed it over.

"Mister Sam, din't recognize you. Good evening!" Blanche looked at Aunt Digna and smiled. Overly warm, Aunt Digna looked anxiously back. Then Blanche stared at Buhlaire a few seconds and merely nodded at her. Made Buhlaire feel like a kid. *I guess that's what I'm supposed to be, too.* All at once, she felt let down. Blanche took Aunt Digna's coat, saying how nice it was. And then: "That's a pretty outfit, honey," she told Buhlaire, and took her coat, too.

"Thanks," Buhlaire said, surprised by the compliment. "My mom got it for me." Then she couldn't think of anything else to say, and she felt stupid.

"She's Bluezy's kid?" Blanche asked, looking at Uncle Sam.

Why don't she ask me?

"This is Miss Buhlaire-Marie Sims, my niece," Uncle Sam said.

Blanche didn't say, "Hi, glad to meet you," or "Hi, Buhlaire." Buhlaire would have been ready with a nice, "Hello, pleased to meet you," back.

Instead, looking at the coat checks she now gave to Uncle Sam, Blanche murmured, "Din't recognize her. She's startin' to look a lot like her dad."

Her words seemed to pull Uncle Sam up tight. He drew back. Unsmiling, he looked at Blanche as if she were some alien type of plant life. She stepped slightly away and fiddled with the coats. Buhlaire could tell she didn't know whether Uncle Sam was finished with her or not.

Uncle Sam marched Aunt Digna and Buhlaire away from Blanche. Buhlaire didn't know how he did that without touching them, but he did. An arm motion showed them that they were to go in front of him. Blanche was left standing in the cold atmosphere Uncle Sam had checked with her.

Act weird about his brother? Like, to mention my dad is an awful way to talk? What is wrong with my dad? Haven't had time to go look for him, but I will. Straight up, I'll ask somebody about him — maybe even Mr. Earl.

Buhlaire sighed and shrugged away thoughts about her father. She felt like enjoying where she was right now. And being in Delmore's was better than anything else they let her do. Maybe being here was so special because it happened only once in a great while. And it was someplace that was for grown-ups and not kids.

The bar was full. It was a big, long bar, with two bartenders and some guy who came in and out with clean glasses and plates. You could get things like popcorn, peanuts, and pretzels, right at the bar.

Uncle Sam looked for their place to sit. He found them one of the banquettes, the upholstered leather benches with curved, built-in seat backs, which lined the mirrored wall across from the bar. Buhlaire got in first, with Aunt Digna next, and Uncle Sam at the other end.

In front of the banquettes were customer tables,

right before the raised bandstand. There was no dance floor. Customers seated in a banquette looked important, was Buhlaire's opinion. She felt proud to be in the very first one next to the bandstand. She sat up straighter when the waitress, all cool in her black slacks and vest uniform, came to take the "Reserved" sign away and get their order.

They had to hurry. To think she could sit right there while Uncle Sam had a beer and Aunt Digna had a pink lady!

The order came pretty fast. Digna telling her, "I can't let you taste it, 'cause you're a minor. They see me giving you a taste and you'll never get to come back. I don't drink it, either. This is just for show."

Oh, sure, Aunt Digna.

Buhlaire had to smile. The waitress brought her a Sprite, half of it poured into a goblet over ice. A little napkin was under the glass. And Aunt Digna told Uncle Sam to order a club sandwich. That even though Buhlaire had just eaten, she was always hungry. So he signaled the waitress and ordered a toasted club with turkey, bacon, and cheese.

When the sandwich came, it was just right, with toothpicks sticking out. It was cut into four parts. Potato chips were on the side, those really good "Mike-sell's" that Buhlaire loved.

Aunt Digna and Buhlaire shared the sandwich. Delicately, they removed the toothpicks. Buhlaire took a big bite. *Ummmm!* Aunt Digna took two dainty bites.

Buhlaire tried not to stare at anybody, the way a little kid might do. But it was clear that some folks looking at her thought she was a little kid and should not be in such a place. *Think I'm going to stay, see my mom with her ostrich-feather fans?* A lump grew in her throat, but it melted as she thought about seeing her mom. Being special in the Sims family.

The place was nearly full. A few people had to stand at the bar. Even though their banquette could seat six, for this set it would hold only Bluezy's folks.

The bartenders recognized her. Looked long and hard at her and Aunt Digna, all dressed up. Even Uncle Sam. Buhlaire vaguely recalled she was here once when she was nine or ten. *I was still asleep then.* She studied her club sandwich and crunched a potato chip between her teeth.

"Use your napkin, baby," Aunt Digna told her, so she did. "We can't stay too long," she added to Uncle Sam.

Uncle Sam sighed. "Digna, we just got here. The set hasn't even started up." He took a long swallow of beer.

"I'm just reminding you this child has school," Digna said.

"We'll stay the set," Uncle Sam said firmly.

Buhlaire grinned and ate her sandwich.

She saw the owner come in — Delilah Moore. *Never looks even anything like her name.* The woman was a mystery with her tight, silk dress with the slits clear up way above her knees. Buhlaire only just now thought about it clearly. *Where has my brain been? She's slim, like a girl.*

She looked at Delilah Moore anew and saw that she was seventy-five if she was a day. Buhlaire recalled that Delilah was said to have a walking stick to match each one of her silk gowns. Tonight she was wearing a shade of wine. Her cane with a pearly knob was lacquered a deep wine, too. She walked, leaning to one side, and heavily on the cane, with one narrow shoulder held higher than the other.

Delilah wore pink rouge high up, starting at the corners of her eyes and coming down to under her cheeks. Her skin looked kind of gray in the soft glow of the club light, and she wore dark maroon lipstick. *Looking like a witch, looking crazy. They say she is half nutty. Oooh, later. Don't let her come over here!*

Delilah Moore made her way with some difficulty around the club. A big guy stayed at her elbow. He was a guard, a bouncer, who made sure no trouble got started. Each time he tried to help Delilah, she snapped at him. People, including Uncle Sam, were chuckling about Delilah's well-known temper. Now they could hear her as she came closer to them. ". . . hover so close on me. Haven't fallen yet. Always think I'm going to fall. Makes me sick."

The bouncer looked embarrassed. It was his job to see that Delilah didn't get upset or too tired. He hoped to convince her to get her driver to take her home in the next half hour.

She came over and pointed her walking stick at Buhlaire. Scared Buhlaire half to death. Buhlaire grabbed Aunt Digna's hand under the table and tried to smile. Aunt Digna squeezed her hand back. Buhlaire knew what that meant. She must stand as best she could in the little space at the table. *Me, standing for all of the Sims family.* She must get up and show respect for Miz Moore's age and position in life. She did get to her feet. And half-standing, Buhlaire said, in the way she knew was proper, "Evening, Miz Delilah. How you doing? I came to see my mom sing."

"Well, that's somethin'," Delilah said. "Nice-lookin' young woman, isn't she?"

Not even a decent hello, how you doing, back.

"Bluezy's baby is growing up. Now the whole bar is looking."

"Don't fill her head with that stuff," Aunt Digna said.

"I bet she knows how pretty she is — don't you, baby?" said Delilah.

"Darlin', how you doing?" Aunt Digna asked Delilah, changing the subject. "How you been? You feeling all right? Haven't seen you lately."

"That's 'cause you all don't come up from the river lately to get some fresh air. Shoot," Delilah said. "How you all stand it down there with all the insects, I'll never know."

Aunt Digna was about to protest, since it was winter and there were no mosquitoes. Buhlaire caught Uncle Sam moving his hand from side to side. A signal for Aunt Digna. Like a head shaking no. Let it pass, is what Uncle Sam meant, Buhlaire decided. Aunt Digna kept still then. She smiled at Delilah as pleasantly as she could. In a minute, Delilah continued around the establishment, greeting patrons with all the tact of a stubborn bulldog.

"She's on her way out," Aunt Digna said matter-of-factly. But her face was set in anger. Uncle Sam made no comment to that. Buhlaire looked at Digna, wondering what she meant.

The house band made its way to the stage — the bass player, the drummer, the keyboardist, and the saxophonist. The keyboardist's name was Kite. He often sang backup for Bluezy. The drummer took off his jacket and spent a long time adjusting his drums.

Then, the bandstand lights lowered. And the soft colored lights came up. Right then, a man's voice said over the P.A. system: "Ladies, gentlemen, good evening. Welcome to Delmore's and this night of delight. Oh, yez! Set yourselves on ready, folks. Here's the great, the one and only, oh, yez! *Bluezy Sims* — all right! Let's give her a hand, folks."

Uncle Sam, clapping, murmured, "Folks will always applaud for Bluezy."

She was there. Her mom. Buhlaire didn't see her come onto the stage from the side. But Bluezy was there, suddenly, like magic, out of the applause. Buhlaire stared and clapped wildly. She began squirming in her seat like some little kid, until Aunt Digna clutched her knee to make her calm down. *Mom! Mom! See me?*

Bluezy Sims knew in a wide glance who all was there. She smiled generally. Gave a lingering look over to the family banquette, and then she pulled the standing mike toward her. Swiftly, one thing happened after another. Buhlaire saw the royal-blue sequined jacket over the powder-blue silk jumpsuit. The outfit set off Bluezy's medium-brown skin, no carrot color anywhere.

Buhlaire watched her face, perfect, with high cheekbones and arched brows. A nose almost tiny. Full lips painted shiny, silky coral-red. Wonderful makeup. I'll never know how to make up like that, Buhlaire thought. Oh, the thrill of it — her mom!

At the keyboard, Kite played a trembly, extended organ note. Then came a thumping, walking-around rhythm and blues. It had a spirited, gospel organ sound to it. At once Buhlaire knew the melody. It was "Bridge Over Troubled Water."

The song had been written way back in 1969 before Buhlaire was born, her mom had told her. It wasn't the kind of up-tempo song Bluezy usually started a set with. But Buhlaire seemed to remember that her mom had started with it once before when Buhlaire had been in the audience. She couldn't separate the words from the music — or herself and her mom from either.

A smile opened Kite's face. For an instant, the light of his eyes found Buhlaire as he began the backup chorus: "*Leave it be, leave it be. Still water runs deep and free.*"

Bluezy came in with her high, edgy voice: "*Yes! Yes-it-does. It does . . .*"

Kite's voice came back, smoothly mellow. He *ab-*

ahhhed up the scale; he let his voice fall and glide down in time, the keyboard switching to a piano melody.

Bluezy came in with a sweet edge at the middle range. It was a caring, gentle tone her mom sang:

> *"When you're weary, feelin' small,*
> *When tears are in your eyes, I'll dry them all;*
> *I'm on your side. Oh, when times get rough*
> *And friends just can't be found,*
> *Like a bridge over troubled water*
> *I will lay me down . . ."*

Kite's voice came, spilling lightness and grace: "*Sail on, silver girl, sail on by.*"

People were applauding, some clapping in time. Buhlaire swallowed hard, blinked back the tears. *Don't cry! Oh, Mommy-mom!*

"*Sail on by,*" Bluezy sang, so sweetly. "*Your time has come to shine. All your dreams are on their way.*"

She and Kite sang together: "*See how they shine.*"

And then, Bluezy, by herself, sang: "*Oh, if you need a friend, I'm sailing right behind. Like a bridge over troubled water.*" Her voice was high and bold.

She and Kite sang: "*I will ease your mind.*"

And finally, Bluezy all alone, singing way up in the air, steely hard and sure: "*Like a bridge over troubled water, I will ease your mind. Darlin', I will ease . . . your . . . mind!*"

The song went on and on inside Buhlaire. Finally, within Delmore's, it came to an end. 'Midst a long applause for Bluezy, Buhlaire thought about the love in the song. It was about her and her mom, caring. But she knew it had been about her mom and dad, once. She wished it were still.

Buhlaire sighed, shook her head with the awesomeness of music. Uncle Sam and Aunt Digna were saying nice things about the song. But she didn't care. Her mom shimmered there under the lights, taking bows.

Has a way of sweeping her arms up and side to side. Like a beautiful mermaid, dancing on the tip of her tail fin. Yeah!

Bluezy had something sparkly in her hair. Her face looked fresh, glowing with the colored lights. There was no sign of sweat shining through her artful stage makeup. Not yet. She was all beauty, all Bluezy Sims, belonging to Buhlaire.

6

Set

Here she was, up late, and, *Snap!* upside down with excitement. Her palms were sweaty. She swallowed a cough. There was such smoke in the air. You could see it. Buhlaire's heart thumped in her ears, throbbing with the music. She tried breathing shallowly, and it seemed to help. Little breaths.

The waitress had taken away Buhlaire's and Uncle Sam's plates. She had long since finished her sandwich. Aunt Digna had finished her pink lady. Never took her eyes off her sister-in-law. Uncle Sam had his back comfortably against the backrest of the banquette. His half-full glass was between his palms, with some folded-up dollar bills between two fingers as he tapped the glass in time. With his eyes closed, he seemed to be watching through his lashes, hearing through his eyelids. Buhlaire studied his face for a long minute, feeling the music go inside her. *Why is it I'm close to him one minute? The next, think he doesn't care for me. Doesn't like Aunt Digna. Then, it changes again. He's my real uncle. Makes me so upset, how things just are liquid, all the time seem flowing away from me.*

They were well along in the set. Bluezy had been

tugging their hearts this way and that. Now her face glistened through the makeup. Her neck was moist. She would be dripping sweat before the set was over.

The piano and drums swung, with a chin-chin-chin on the cymbals. It was an outright blues number, minor sounding, talking about bad news. *Rhythm of it — you could even waltz to it, step, step-step.*

Bluezy and the saxophone came in just before the second step.

> *"People all around me —*
> *I don't even have a friend.*
> *Lord knows I been tryin'*
> *And he knows I just can't win.*
> *Everything I do seems to turn out wrong.*
> *Sometimes I wish that I'd never been born."*

Kite began singing backup to Bluezy in a very nice, high-pitched falsetto voice: "*Seems like nobody, nobody cares.*"

Bluezy came in: "*Lonely nights, you know, I've had my share. It just ain't fair. No, it's not. It ain't fair.*"

People were singing along with Bluezy, clapping softly in time. No longer just customers, they were Bluezy's partners, moving in rhythm in their seats. Buhlaire found she was holding her breath. She remembered the last verse now, and, always, her part in it:

"Some folks have it easy
And live a life of fun and play.
Lord knows I struggle and struggle,
Trying to make my way.
But one of these old days,
I'm going to reach the top.
I believe, I hope I can make it,
'Cause Buhlaire won't let me stop . . ."

Buhlaire grinned from ear to ear, couldn't help herself, and clutched one hand in the other under the table. Folks applauded, saying, "Yes, indeed!"

Bluezy sang and sang. She must've sung eight or nine songs when Aunt Digna seemed to get a little nervous and told Uncle Sam, "Getting to be about that time."

"No, it's early yet," Uncle Sam said.

"Come on, Sam, she's got school."

"This'll be better for her than any school."

"You can't mean that. Look at people, they're having too much . . . She doesn't need be around . . ." And then, "I'm just afraid he — "

" — Digna," Sam interrupted. "You are always afraid for nothing. Let up, will you?"

But it was almost over. Buhlaire saw her mom looking at them. She had ended one song. The wild clapping had subsided. The musicians were shifting around, wiping their faces, hands. Bluezy was given a towel, with which she gently dabbed at her forehead.

"Almost done-time, folks," she said, generally.

And people at the bar protested. Bluezy went on, "But before we finish singing, I'd like you to meet someone's got a *voice*! Come on up here, baby."

Everybody got quiet. Bluezy was looking right at her. "Buhlaire, get yourself up here!" People laughed, surprised, and applauded.

Uncle Sam laughed. "See? See?" he said to a shocked Digna. Before Digna could think of anything to say, Uncle Sam was on his feet and letting Buhlaire out on his side. Buhlaire was transfixed by her mother standing there. When she was out in the aisle, everybody started applauding her, saying things: "I didn't know she could . . . did you know she sang?" Interested, they were willing to listen to her.

She was scared inside, excited inside, and practically numb and dumbstruck all over. Her mom, calling her up there! Sure, they'd sung together. Many times, at home. But up there!

And Buhlaire remembered when she was real little, singing before a crowd. She'd loved the Beatles' songs. But she couldn't remember where that was. Was that in a club like this one?

Sure, they could harmonize. *Mom goes, "You got the highest voice, you sing the top, Buhlaire."* Were they going to sing her favorite for harmonizing? *Oh, Mom!*

When she was right down front facing her mom, she could feel the lights. Bluezy gave her a hand up the foot-high platform. *Mommy!*

Bluezy, holding her close a minute, whispered in her ear, "Now don't be scared. Just do it the way we always do. You don't *even* have to think about it."

She looked in her mom's face. Loved her and squeezed her.

"Turn around now, face the crowd," her mom said.

The way we're dressed? A fleeting thought. All in blue, both of us — know we look like an *act*! My clothes! You did that on purpose!

"Folks, meet 'the voice.' This is my li'l love, my daughter, Buhlaire."

Buhlaire faced them, heard their applause for her. She couldn't see anything, at first. She wasn't used to the stage lights in her eyes. But then she figured out how to look through them and managed to see a little better. Thank goodness she couldn't see Aunt Digna's face over in the banquette. Oh, but she could feel her *eyes*!

Then Bluezy half turned to Kite. At once, Buhlaire knew the song. Now, she let her own voice set the song's stage:

> *"When I find myself in times of trouble,*
> *Mother Mary comes to me*
> *Speaking words of wisdom*
> *Let it be."*

Kite sang softly in his falsetto, almost in a whisper:

> *"Oh, let it be."*

Buhlaire and Bluezy sang together, with Buhlaire's voice way on top of her mom's, and as tight as a silken coat covering Bluezy:

> *"And in my hour of darkness*
> *She is standing right in front of me.*
> *Speaking words of wisdom*
> *Let it be."*

Buhlaire and Kite sang the chorus. Then she and Bluezy sang in sweet harmony:

> *"And when broken-hearted people*
> *Living in a world of dreams*
> *There will be an answer —"*

And Kite came in with:

> *"Let it be."*

Next, Buhlaire and Bluezy sang, softly, softly. And Buhlaire, to herself, *Don't think! Oh, just listen for Mom, sound, don't think! Don't you cry!*

Buhlaire sang, high and sweet, with a gentle piano. She almost lost her concentration when her mind wandered for an instant, but she held herself with all her strength, and stayed in control:

> *"And when the night is cloudy*
> *There is still a light that shines on me — "*

Folks burst out with, "Yes! Beautiful!" and applause. Her voice, trembling with hope:

> *"Shines until tomorrow*
> *Let it be, let it be!"*

She was on the very edge of the child she had been. But she did not fall back into that tender, frightened, little self. They finished in harmony, she and Kite and Bluezy, with the saxophone, piano, and drums:

> *"I wake up to the sound of music*
> *Mother Mary comes to me*
> *Speaking words of wisdom*
> *Let it be.*
> *Let it be, let it be, let it be, let it be.*
> *Whisper words of wisdom, let it be."*

There was so much love and life, class, in the sound of them.

Somewhere in the midst of the last, stirring verse, Bluezy suddenly broke off. Kite left off in the third line. Buhlaire clung to a high note and, like falling from a tightwire, she let go of it. Something happened. It was as if their voices had plunged down a well of silence. The audience had disappeared.

Suddenly Buhlaire was conscious of a hand there amid the stage lights' glow. It moved ever so slowly up through the colored lights toward her. She stared at a hand, wrist, part of a forearm. The hand was shot through with tiny quiverings. The wrist was thin and pale. She recognized these parts of somebody in a swift, piecing-together of what she saw.

Buhlaire had no time to think what the hand reaching toward her might mean.

At her side, Bluezy hissed. All at once, big, burly shoulders came into the light. Bouncer shoulders. A thick hand and sleeve of a suit caught hold of the wrist with the trembly hand that had first entered the colored spots. The bouncer's arm came across, and the wrist and hand were taken out of the light. *Who was it?* The blinding stage light didn't allow her to see the rest of the person.

That was all, then. Only a line of music had fallen out of their singing. Only a small mistake. The crowd had grown silent. But Bluezy was right there, bringing the music back with her. She was there again on the *Let it be*'s.

Buhlaire came in on the second *Let it be*, and it sounded just right:

> "*Let it be, let it be, let it be,*
> *let . . . it . . . be . . .*
> *Whisper words of wisdom, let it be. . . .*"

There was a swelling of murmurs, of approval. Then the crowd applauded loudly for a long time. Over that came the announcer's voice: "Folks, Bluezy Sims, Bluezy and the band. Bluezy Sims, folks. And give a hand to Little Bluezy, Toozy. Yeah! Oh, yez!"

People smiled at Buhlaire. She felt their love as she came down from the stage. Maybe later they'd think about the lapse that had happened, the hand out of nowhere. It meant little after such a good set.

The stage lights came up as Kite announced the end of the set. Before long, the band was ready to depart. Bluezy left without a fuss, through the rear door.

Buhlaire was once again with Uncle Sam and Aunt Digna. She felt very tired, nerves jangling. She was even too moved, too tightly strung, to speak for a moment. *Guess so are Uncle Sam and Aunt Digna.* Strange how they looked at her. Like the music and her singing set her apart from them. *Just like with Mom. She is apart, too. What does it mean, that the music does that? I'll ask Mom one time.*

Inside herself, she felt a glow. She felt wonderful. She'd done her part of the singing perfectly. *Pretty cool! Straight up, I didn't make not one mistake. Mom was proud of me. All the musicians, they think I can be good like Mom. Boy, oh boy! Girl, oh girl! Man, oh man! I did it!*

Outside, the winter night was again upon them. It had started to snow, in a fine dusting, blown in on a bitter wind. Uncle Sam and Aunt Digna walked in front of her. She heard snatches of their conversation. Aunt Digna: "Going up there . . . scared me . . . didn't know what he'd . . ."

Uncle Sam: "It was her. He'd never do any . . ."

Aunt Digna: "He could've . . . you never know . . . please, get him . . . you could make him . . ."

"This is his . . . no matter . . . he'd come . . ."

"But . . . to protect her from . . ."

"I say let . . . it's her . . . she knows . . ."

Buhlaire listened as hard as she could. It dawned on her then that the hand in the light might've been her dad's. *My dad, come to see me?* The thought slowed her down. Pleased and excited her. She knew Aunt Digna wanted to keep her dad away from her. It seemed that Uncle Sam was saying: Let it alone. *Let it be! And my dad's supposed to be dead!*

It was in the middle of the night, she woke up, hearing the moaning trees. Smelling perfume. Not really, but dreaming she did. And probably hearing her mom, that was what woke her. Her mom was home. Half asleep, Buhlaire listened for her mom to settle in. Then, after a time, she went to her mom's bedroom. Crept in and into her bed, just the way she'd always done since she was a child, alone. Her mom, with her back to her, breathing long and deep.

"Mom."

"Ummh." Not turning, not moving.

"Can I come in?" She snuggled close against her mom's back.

"Wait," Bluezy mumbled, and painfully turned herself over.

When she was over, Buhlaire arranged herself snug in her mom's lap.

"You're all warm," she said.

"Ummh," said her mom.

"Are you very tired?"

"Too weak, talk," her mom said.

"Are you sick?"

"Um-um."

"Did I do good?"

"Um-hum. Did very good."

"Thanks — did you dance?"

Her mom stiffened, suddenly alert, and awake. "Yes, I did." When Buhlaire stayed quiet, her mom said, "It's like singing. It's what I do."

"I know," Buhlaire said. *But I don't like it. Maybe if you let me see it.* "Hey!" she added, craning her neck around at her mom. She turned on her stomach.

"Buhlaire!"

"But if you danced for me sometime, in your . . . swim suit? Then I'd know what it was like. And then I could tell kids they're stupid."

"Buhlaire." Her mom sighed.

That meant her mom probably would dance sometime for her. Buhlaire snuggled back into her mom's lap. *What bothers me, though — I never did ever ask her to dance before. Because I was little. Because I thought a fan-dance was a bad kinda dance? Well, it doesn't have to be. It's my mom and what she does. It's like singing. Called an art. So there.*

"Mom. . . ." Whispering.

"Oh, God — Buhlaire, I am exhausted. Please — "

"Okay, sorry. I'll be quiet. But I love you."

Her mom giggled. "But I love you back." And then Bluezy was out, fast asleep, snoring softly down on her baby's ear.

7

Her Dad

Rasta tangles spread out under her cheek against the pillow. Twisted strands covered her nose as she slept. Her hair reeked of night-old cigarette smoke out of Delmore's. The odor made her cough awake with a stale, unpleasant taste on her tongue.

Her dad was on her mind even before she opened her eyes. Then, seeing the room, it took her a minute to figure out where she was.

Oh. Mom's bedroom. She let the memory of being so close and comfortable with her mom wash over her. The recollection was sweet — snuggling warm in her mom's arms, and their brief, private talking.

She swung her legs out of bed and sat there, looking at the floor, as the night before at Delmore's came into view behind her eyes. All the singing with her mom had been just the greatest. And then, what had happened right before the end of the set: *Sure, it was. Whose hand in the lights. Him, standing there. Oh, my own dad come to see me! I bet it was.*

All of them, so mean. Keeping him from me? I hate them!

Buhlaire thought about her mom again and looked

around. *Where is she?* "Mom?" She listened, hearing a faint movement. "I got a meat-bone to pick with you!"

Rushing out into the hall, she met Aunt Digna coming from the living room. "Mom!" Buhlaire hollered at the top of her lungs. Digna stood in her path, staring at her. The smell of coffee drifted in from the kitchen, made Buhlaire hungry. Her mom never answered. Buhlaire felt anger start dripping inside her, like the coffee percolating, getting stronger.

"Bluezy had to go," Digna said. "Told me to tell you she'd talk to you on the phone this evening, or tomorrow from" — she turned away — "somewhere, maybe it was Columbus. I forget. I'm suppose to remember all the sadiddy places she loves to go to? And good morning to you, too, Miss Buhlaire, noisy this morning."

Buhlaire swore right in Aunt Digna's face. "This family is some sickening mess, you know?" She swore again, spitting bad words out into the air. It surprised her how easily they came. Her eyes were accusing. Digna was a stand-in for her mom who'd left her again, and without a kiss or a good-bye. Without a good word.

Digna's arm moved as if a sudden wind lifted it. A swift, burning slap brought Buhlaire to her knees. She'd missed seeing the hand that hit her, but the pain caused her to crumble. She howled and glared through gushing tears at Aunt Digna standing over her.

Digna looked stunned at what she'd done; nevertheless, she said, "Don't you never ever curse at me. Why, the very idea! You never use that kind of language in this house. Never!"

Trying to help Buhlaire up, she said, "You know I'm sorry. But a twelve-year-old talking like that! I don't care if you are big for your age. What comes from a mother doesn't know how nor when to be one."

Buhlaire pushed Digna away with a vicious shove, and scooted back along the floor. "You ugly old bag!" she cried, outraged. "Don't you touch me, you, you — !" Looking deadly, she said a word she knew she never should have uttered the moment it was out of her mouth.

Aunt Digna Sims came after her. This time, her hitting hand made a fist. But before she ever reached Buhlaire, Aunt Babe was there. Hearing the commotion, Babe had come swiftly through the door from her rooms. She wrapped her arms around Digna from behind and held on, taking Digna by surprise. "Don't hit that child! You don't abuse that baby!" she said.

"Let go of me, you crazy woman!" Digna shouted. "Let me go, I said!"

"Just be still a minute and sit yourself down," Aunt Babe answered, panting.

"How'm I going to sit down with you holding on to me?" Digna asked. "I said, let me go!" Digna held her breath, trying to force her muscles out hard to break Babe's hold. She couldn't break it. She swung herself this way and that; still, Babe clung to her, swinging around with her.

They struggled in their awful dance before Buhlaire's stricken eyes. They circled the living room, once, twice. Their legs got tangled. They knocked against the dining table, then fell hard into an easy chair, Digna on Babe's lap.

Buhlaire wanted to laugh at how stupid two grown women looked pitted against one another. Yet it made her want to cry to see how quickly her household had turned into some ugly place.

Just because I got mad at Mom I had to go swear at Aunt Digna. Only, I didn't mean it at her. "Don't, you all," she said softly. Seeing her aunts at war, she had an awful feeling, like somebody close had got hurt bad. "Please." She could hardly get the words out. "Stop it, you all."

Aunt Babe heard her. Babe couldn't tell for certain where the whisperings came from. She couldn't quite see Buhlaire through the shadows that lived in her own eyes. But in her loving heart, she heard that soft, little voice. She released Digna. Her last strength was about gone, anyway.

"Get off me," she told Digna. She could hardly get her breath.

Furious, Digna struggled out of Babe's lap and flung herself away. Turning on Babe, she shouted, "You hold me down like that again, and you don't know what may happen to you!" Her face looked bitter. Digna came close, bent over Babe, poking her in the shoulder with each word.

"Stop it, Digna, that hurts!" Babe exclaimed.

"You'll hurt more than that if you ever interfere with me again. I didn't do wrong to Buhlaire," Digna went on. "I taught her a lesson was what I did."

"I'll tell Sam," Babe said. "It's child abuse, and I saw it."

"Hush up! Blind old fool, you can't see nothing," she said. "It was a lesson, and she knows it."

"What lesson does the child witness this minute? Tell me that," Babe asked.

"Right now she's watching a blind fool who couldn't see straight even if she *could* see something, which it's clear she can't," Digna said.

The two of them kept up their quarreling. Aunt Babe saw movement to the side, as Buhlaire slowly inched around until she was out of the room. Babe kept Digna occupied the whole time so Buhlaire could get free.

When Digna noticed Buhlaire had gone, she looked relieved. But she seemed let down, done in by her own pent-up true feelings — anger at Bluezy for causing the child hurt. And being upset herself at having to see Buhlaire being hurt. So many feelings, so long, and under the tightest control.

Buhlaire stood silently, listening from the doorway of her room.

"Don't know what got into me," Digna said, "hitting the child like that."

Babe was silent a moment before she said, finally, "I know you didn't mean to. You were provoked. But, still . . ." She let the thought go.

Digna sighed shakily. She gave another long, raggedy sound, angry at Bluezy, tired of her own dull life. She left the room, scuffing her shoes on the carpet, too upset to lift up her feet.

Exhausted, Aunt Babe leaned back in the chair and closed her eyes. She'd once told Buhlaire that behind her eyelids was a gray sightlessness. Said she enjoyed watching it. That it was a pleasant feeling to be pulled into the gray depths. "You ought to see it," she'd said. "It's like floating in a warm spring fog."

Now Buhlaire was in her room, getting dressed and ready to go. She was thinking: Nobody, nobody cares.

Last night, the song was word up. Truth. No, not anybody. What about Aunt Babe? She tried. Still, it was just to save me from what she calls abuse. But nobody. Mom sure acts like she don't. My dad? Mom. Dad. Come and go.

Suddenly, sobs broke in her throat. *They don't want me?* It was an awful thought that made her gush bitter tears. The next moment, the crying disappeared. But the mournful feeling wouldn't leave her. It came to her mind that caring about loved ones, and what happened to you when you did, could be just like dying. *So. Let it be.*

All I know is, I have to get out of here. She put on the white jumpsuit. *Must've washed it again after I took it off yesterday — Aunt Digna. And brought it in here this morning.* She felt cold, dead, thinking about her aunt now.

Buhlaire put on her heavy wool socks and her shoes, then her boots. Boots, made clean and bright by Aunt Digna. *Huh. Thinks I can't do it myself, or that I'll forget.* She made sure she had her gloves and took up her bookbag. She remembered she had homework left undone. She hurried to the kitchen, had a cup of coffee and some toast, started some homework but didn't finish it. She went back to her room, feeling undecided about whether to go to school.

Out her window, it looked windy and snowy. She took a minute to think, spinning around. Room didn't look like much. She always made her bed as soon as she got up. She'd slept in it part of the night last night, so she straightened it up now.

There was nothing on her walls other than Navajo white paint. No pictures hanging or anything. There was nothing on her dresser or lamp table as you might find in other girls' rooms. Aunt Digna had all brushes and mirrors kept neatly in a bathroom cupboard. Oh, you could take a comb and brush, stand before your own dresser mirror with them, but you had to bring them back so they could be kept all together. Aunt Digna did not like hair strands floating in the air and falling on the carpet. She did not like leaving articles on dressers — perfumes, brushes, combs, powders. Jewelry, especially. "They tend to disappear," she told Buhlaire once.

Does she mean she thinks I take stuff? Has stuff disappeared, or did Aunt Digna put it all away? Why didn't I ever notice this before? Buhlaire couldn't answer anything anymore.

* * *

Buhlaire had seen other kids' rooms, and now she thought about it. Bunch of kids after a game. They'd go over to somebody's house for Kool-Aid, lemonade, maybe some sandwiches. Once in a great while, Sandy would let Buhlaire tag along with her. Nobody would say anything, as long as she was with Sandy. Somebody's mom who was home every single day and never went far away would be there. A dad would be in the house, too, even though he might not be the real father of a kid. He'd still come home while all of them were there. Buhlaire always managed to hang close to some kid's big dad, in the living room and in the kitchen, too. She couldn't get enough of seeing how some dad acted.

And some kids' rooms would have all kinds of things all over the place. Events programs, goalie gloves. How was it some kids could keep their stuff together, and she couldn't? Sandy had a tray made of mirror glass on her dresser. And on the mirror tray was really cool stuff, brushes, combs, lipstick. A ring holder. A necklace rack. A velvet bow. Little pearl barrettes. Good stuff that Buhlaire never seemed to have out on her dresser. It was funny. She kept a few things like that in the top drawer of her dresser on one side, in a small cardboard box Aunt Digna had given her. Her mom's and Digna's rooms were empty the same way.

Things — I never even noticed before. Pictures of teams. Class pictures and pictures of friends. Them, kids, with their friends. Them, at school picnics.

Why didn't somebody ever take her picture, just by herself, she wondered. Let me hang it on my wall or put it on my dresser?

She was in the group photo of basketball and Chorus. But she didn't own one of the pictures. Maybe her mom kept them somewhere — Buhlaire didn't know. But nobody took her picture and put a caption under it. Like, "Buhlaire dances on her toes." Or, "Buhlaire sleeping in study hall." The way there were captions under pictures of pretty girls. Wasn't she supposed to be pretty? Delilah Moore had thought so. *Wonder why I thought of me as Buhlaire, dancing. I don't dance. Mom does. Do I have to do what she does? No, I don't. I don't have to sing, either, if I don't want to.*

Maybe I don't count. Grady . . . thinks I do.

The thought made her move. Maybe five minutes had passed. She had to get out now. She thought of going out the window. It wasn't hard to do. Then she thought she wouldn't, as anger flared again.

Who am I? Who am I?

She went to find Aunt Digna. The door to Digna's room was open halfway. She pushed it wide and stood there, not going into the room. Saw Aunt Digna seated in her chair, with her head on her hand. Digna made no move, except to open her eyes, stare toward the floor.

"I don't say bad words, and you don't hit me," Buhlaire said. "Don't you hit me ever again, or I'll go live with my dad."

Digna jumped up. Her face just seemed to freeze

in fear. Buhlaire closed the door as hard as she could. She didn't slow down, even when Aunt Babe called her name from the living room.

She was ready to go, bookbag on her shoulder. She was out of the house. In her mind, she locked sadness in that house, where it couldn't get her.

Oh!

Everything was free and different outside. There was a droning sound of nature, high up in the branches. Like the trees all around were a chorus, helping out a gale of wind. Everything was so very white. White sky, white land. Mist, foggy low clouds that had a snowblink. *I know about that!* She remembered as she scanned the underbelly of fat, dark clouds. The snowblink, the shiny bright underside of the clouds, was caused by the reflection of the light off the snow lands.

Ooooh! She loved the snow in her face. Instantly, the cold made her more wide awake, more alert. Her legs were moving, just like they knew where to go. She was striding in fast time, and it felt so good to be out.

Where do I go? She thought of Uptown, as she would when she was striding from the river toward town. *Too far, too cold.* Oh, it was cold! Snow streamed on a wind, on a slant. It would stop with a wind gust. Something about the moisture in the air and the cold made things appear suddenly smokey before her eyes. If she could only see herself! *Bet I'm all invisible, too.*

I'll see Uptown in summer, when I look there for a job.

Lots-a jobs in Uptown. Lots-a money and people wanting things done for them. I've got enough money now to go practically anywhere. About four-hundred smack-a-roos, bwoy!

Am I going to school now? She swung around to the edge of Midway. The school campus was situated between it and Uptown. To her right about a quarter of a mile away was Montgomery Park. She circled around, fell in behind bunches of kids going to school. Far enough away so that she could slip on beyond school grounds with no trouble. Cut through Montgomery Park's far limit, behind the hills for sledding. One minute, she was in the crowd going. The next minute, she was out of their sight.

Guess I'm not going. At least, skip this morning.

She didn't know exactly when Grady began following her. But after she turned away from the school grounds, all at once, she knew he was there.

Like some hunt-dog on my trail! Must've been waiting for me. Can you believe it? And not even twenty-four hours since I poured the milk on him. Seems like a week! Sooo much has happened.

Grady must've been somewhere out of her sight, but where he could see her when she kept on going. *Must've been the way it was.* She didn't know whether or not she was glad he was there.

Something's changed — I went into Aunt Digna's room and said what I did. I can go with my dad! All at once, she realized she didn't have to stay in that house. A rush of warm feeling came over her, made her smile. *That's it, too. That's for real!*

When she passed Midway's variety store, she turned the corner. She walked toward Shelter From *Any* Storm, the hostelry for the poor and homeless. She stopped in front, looking through the closed double doors. Boldly, she opened them and went in. She didn't think about it. It was something she had to do.

Her dad would surely have a home somewhere. But maybe he would stop here for a reason she didn't know about. *His brothers are upset with him about something. Else, why wouldn't Uncle Sam want him around?*

She strode into the lobby like she knew what she was doing, had to meet somebody. But her heart was pounding. People were around, shuffling this way and that. The shelter had lots of room. She had an impression of a rounded space. Columns, and long corridors. It was an old building, made over, and used for people with no place else to be.

A man sat behind a desk. He was busy with some people hovering around him. He missed seeing Buhlaire hurry through. She went on, following the sound of a large number of voices. She went into another room, more like a hall. It was so huge. Row upon row of long tables. People busy serving food. A large, ragtag crowd was seated at the tables, finishing their breakfasts. At the far end of the room, a door was open, and an overflowing line of people was coming through to be taken care of by the servers. There had to be a couple hundred seated. Really poor people, looking sleepy and sad. She even walked near the moving line a moment. But she didn't see anybody who might belong to her. Be her dad.

Don't know how I can ask about him. She tried to imagine what he would be like. Stopped to think, but didn't dare stand there too long. Moving, she took a swift glance around the room. So many people looking so worn out! She couldn't imagine her dad would live in a place like this. Odors of decay and unclean bodies. She was glad she didn't see anyone who looked like he might be related to her.

People sitting on orange or aqua plastic bucket chairs. Somebody was watching her. A little kid! He came over, started walking with her. Then another, bigger kid sidled up. "He thinks you look like our mom," said the bigger one. "You do, kinda. He's my brudder."

What? A guard slowly made his way along the moving chow line from the rear of the room toward the front. In a minute, he was going to be right up with her. Maybe he was going to ask her what she was doing there. Her heart skipped a beat.

"Mommy?" said the little kid to her. Funny little face, turned way up to see her. He had a slice of bread in his hand, all folded up and gooey. The bigger one laughed. "You stupid!" he said to his little brother.

Kids were usually surprised by the way she looked — her light, Rasta hair, her skin color, and her eyes. The little kid tried to hold her hand with his sticky fingers. Round, black eyes looking longingly at her. The bigger kid was watching her to see what she would do. She turned abruptly on her heel and walked away. The bigger kid snickered. "Commere, dumb doo-doo," he said to his little brother, who had started to follow her.

Snap! Outside, Buhlaire didn't look around for Grady. But in a few minutes, she figured it was the shape of him she saw out of the corner of her eye. She didn't have time to think about him.

The whole place, shelter, and her own gumption, surprised her. Probably an apartment building once, she thought, with yellow walls and old-fashioned design stuff on them. It had a funky odor. It was a place she didn't know about. It fed people, though, she'd seen that much. People went there, and it kept them penned up, she didn't know about safe. *That little kid needed folks, like I need my dad. Mom.*

It upset her, the way kids were left someplace. *Like, leaving them alone is okay, 'long as they're warm and have some food — it's not okay!*

Seeing so many homeless people made her think that maybe her own family could be homeless. *Aunt Babe, without a clue!* It scared her; then, it made her angry. It wasn't right. Old people. Kids. *Feel like throwing my bookbag away. Just give it up.* No, she would keep her bookbag, but she wouldn't go to school at all today, she decided. Maybe not again, if she went away with her dad. *If I don't go walking, I'll scream.*

Her dad had to be someplace, but she was still afraid to ask anybody. Scared to death to say to somebody, "Have you seen my dad? I can't tell you what he looks like 'cause I don't know myself."

People would think I was dumb. She had her pride, too.

My dad. Maybe she could go to school and have a talk with Mr. Earl about him. But somehow it shamed her to have to ask somebody who wasn't even her family where her own dad was.

She felt so blue inside. She went on, with her head down, hunched deep in her shoulders.

A half mile out of town, she ran into blowing snow. She could hear the highway. Cars and trucks, slowly making their way on the icy four-lane. The snow was falling, too, stinging, coming on a slant across the interstate. She couldn't see the cars, just maybe dark lumps far off and moving. *Aunt Babe's shadows!* Everything was so wet and cold!

And then, she did something unexpected. She didn't know she would do it until she was about to. But there was some devilment in her. She turned around and started striding back. She broke into a short run, sliding, keeping her balance. She ran near Grady, shadow — she could almost see him. *Snow shadow!* Buhlaire felt this strength in herself, excitement at him, following her still.

She shouted "Whoo-oo!" like she was part of the snow-stormy sounds. "You don't know me, Grady!" she shouted. Her voice carried on wind-streams.

"I'm not sorry what I did, either." Talking about spilling her milk on him. "Why do you follow me? You hate me!" *No, you don't — do you?* "I hate you!"

"Buhlaire? Buhlaire!" she heard him call. Hard to hear him with her breath in her ears and the wind. "Wait! Buhlaire!" he called.

But she shouted more. "You're just the same as everybody." *You don't know what it's like for me.* "Go on, get outta here, bwoy." *'Fore you get yourself lost.* "Go on back!"

"Buhlaire . . . I'm . . . not . . . only . . ."

Blasts of wind and snow kept taking his voice away. She turned and strode swiftly from him. She saw the gray lumps moving at a slow rate on the interstate. Telephone poles, trees, no longer had any height. They were shrunken posts guarding the frigid landscape.

Her cheeks had turned to ice. Her feet were going numb. *Awful out here. Colder than I thought.* Blowing snow caked her Rasta twists. Ice coated her lashes so she could hardly see.

Blind, me? Aunt Babe! Aunt Babe!

8

Underpass

Buhlaire moved like a patch of gray shade through sweeping snow. She'd turned away from where she'd had her little talk with Grady. *Snap!* Now she was parallel to the interstate above her on the right. To prove she wasn't scared, she would go in closer to it. Then, she'd veer left toward the way she'd come. Just a nice walk, she told herself. She didn't know what would happen after that. She couldn't think that far.

She could feel her bookbag below her shoulder, frozen now in a load on her back. *Never mind!* The sounds of trucks groaning and cars straining seemed to be calling her. She kept peering upward through the snowfall. All those sounds were teasing her. *Like to go up there. I must be crazy, to be out here! Didn't know it was so bad out*. Abruptly, she turned, putting her back to the highway. *What'll I do? I can't go home.* Cold wind and snow hit her across her back now. Strong gusts were like huge hands, pushing her. She could still see the shapes of trees, and the interstate, like a giant serpent slithering over the land.

But weather had its own way. Right before her

eyes, it got worse. The snow all but stopped. She always knew there could be swift change out here. Snowfields for as far as she could see were a wide plain. *Plain City!* Sleet, ice storms could come out of nowhere.

You'd think it'd get better when the snow stopped. All at once, the day flooded with radiance. Buhlaire felt as if she were growing small. As if she were way inside the light, a rice kernel on snow white.

Trouble.

Up and down and to the sides. It seemed as if all of a sudden, blinding light was everywhere in a deadly, glowing white. *I'm in trouble!* Snowfields, clouds, shadow-trees, poles, melted into space, and were gone.

Whiteout! Her insides flashed with fear.

School taught about snow and freezing. High wind could carry snow in a blinding blizzard. Kids knew to stay close to home when winds rode on winter weather. But whiteout could happen in wide, quiet reaches of snow. She'd never seen it and had never been in it. She hadn't guessed it would happen to her out here. Nothing had been further from her mind.

Sunlight filtering through low-hanging clouds reflected off the snowfields. It bounced back up to the clouds again in a deadly turnaround. Everything became the same level of brightness. The landscape was wiped away in cold, white brilliance.

Only thing is light!

Cars and trucks that had been crawling along the

interstate ground to a halt, motors running still. Horns began blowing wildly, warning other cars.

Buhlaire stopped dead in her tracks. Her eyes were open as wide as the gusts of wind and snowfall would allow, and she still couldn't see. *Oh, why'd I do this dumbness?* It was worse out than being closed in fog, or blowing snow. *I don't know where I am. Yes, you do. You know the interstate is behind. Oh, don't panic. You're not lost.* It felt as if the white was tracking her down, that danger was just outside it. Something awful could get her.

She started running. "Oooh, somebody!" she cried out. "Oh, please, somebody come!" She knew she shouldn't run. But she panicked. And when she tripped on something and slipped, and fell hard on her hip, she got up slowly. She was shaking now with the cold, snow down her neck, and she was blinded.

"Somebody! Help!" It felt as if she couldn't get enough air. "Help, I'm lost! Help me!" It was just the hardest, aching fall. "Help!" she gasped.

The bright white slammed into her. It was like being at the bottom of everything white pressing down on her. She tried to see so hard, her eyes began to ache. She closed them to stop the pain. *Can't see. Can't see anything!* She began to cry and couldn't stop.

"Buhlaire!"

What? "Help! Grady! Grady!"

"Buhlaire, I'm coming!"

"Oh, great!" *Thank you. Thank you!* She scrambled to her feet.

"Don't move! I can't see!" He was getting closer.

"Over here!" she said. "Over here! Over here!"

He took her hand. That quickly, he was beside her. He took her arm.

"Oh, we're lost. We're in trouble," she said, sobbing. "I don't know where we are."

"I know where we are," somebody said, right in her ear.

All went still; all went cold inside her. The voice was a voice she didn't know. *Oh, please.* It wasn't Grady's voice! *Who?* "Hey, let go of me!" She tried to break away, but whoever it was held on. "Hey, who are you? You better let me go!"

Maybe the bad-news stranger she'd run into back at the Water Houses yesterday. Just yesterday! she thought fleetingly.

"Buhlaire, it's okay. I can get you out of here."

"Huh?"

"Open your eyes, see if you can see me. Don't be afraid of me. I'm your daddy."

It took a long, long time to sink in. *What? Daddy?* "My . . . dad?" *Where's Gra — ?* She couldn't move. She was shaking all over from the cold and from fear.

But the sound of him! *My dad! No, you're not! My dad's . . .* Something about his voice made her do what he said. She opened her eyes. She held her breath. Felt that if she even breathed, he'd be some kind of fantastic dream she'd made up to save herself.

My dad? My dad. My dad. Can you believe, my dad?

She had to squint, but she could see him. She had a good quick look at his hair, Rastas, just like hers, caked with snow. He wore a scarf loosely over the top of his head that wound down across his mouth and jaw. It, too, was snow-covered. But she'd seen his eyes and nose. She'd seen his skin color. A pale yellow glow. A honeyed vanilla. Where'd she hear that? Aunt Digna saying . . .

There was something about the way he looked at her. He had to be who he said he was. She was closer than she ever remembered being to a dad. He gazed at her in such a way that she thought maybe he did belong to her.

"Thought you were — " She couldn't finish.

"Thought I was — dead. That's what they told you," he said. "Didn't they? She said she would."

"I thought you were this . . . this boy from my school. Grady Terrell," she said.

"He's been following you," said her dad. He took a moment to put sunglasses on.

The next thing, Grady was right there with them, led by the sound of their voices. He was snow-covered and shivering the way she was. "I can't see much," he said.

"Says he's my dad," Buhlaire said shyly. She felt odd, like she could fall asleep on her feet.

"Know him, too. Seen him before out here," Grady said.

Following me?

"Listen, Grady," said her dad. "I'm holding her

arm, and you can hold the other one. You help me, and I can get us out of here."

What was he called? "You're Junior. Junior Sims," she said. *My dad!*

"Yeah, that's me," he said. "I'm your daddy!" He laughed loudly. It began to snow on them again.

Buhlaire felt weak and deeply tired. "I'm so sleepy, all a-sudden," she said.

"Freezing yourself out here," Junior, her dad, said. "Even your tears are frozen." He laughed again. It sounded empty. "Need to get y'all outta the cold."

Something strange, yet sweet-sounding, about him, she thought. His voice was slow and easy, full of summer sun. *Daddy* . . . She'd waited so long. But now, for some reason, she felt let down. And if she could just lie still, she could figure out why she didn't care so much about her dad being with her right now. She just didn't.

She felt cozy, all wrapped up deep inside herself. Like snow, the thought *this is how you freeze* came drifting down on her. She was too tired. She couldn't feel anything much. Not even the cold now. "Did it get warmer?" she asked.

"Walk," her dad said. "It's not far. I can build up the fire, and you'll be warm."

Now she could feel they were moving. She could feel Grady on one side of her. Had hold of her arm. She could hear him breathing, straining against the weather. She jerked her arm just to show him she was still Buhlaire. She hardly moved it. He held on.

"I've got my eyes closed," she said.

"It's better now. You can open them a little at a time," her dad said.

She opened her eyes. She couldn't wipe the snow out of her lashes. Junior, her dad, holding her by the arm, had his other arm across her back. *My dad's alive. He's got me.* "You have been following me, too," she said.

"Yeah," he said. "We'll talk in a little while." He laughed nervously.

The laugh, softer now, sounded odd. Buhlaire couldn't get what it all meant. She shook her head. Had to close her eyes again. "I'm dizzy," she said.

She could clearly hear the interstate. They were closer to it than she'd ever been. "Are we going up there? You're going to take me away — " she said to her dad.

"We're going to go under it," he said. "But you can come with me, if you want to." He laughed, a cold sound. "You shouldn't even come out here — you got toughs all over the place out here."

"I never see anybody," she murmured.

"You don't see them, not unless they wanna be seen," he said. "They see you. I saw you."

"I saw *you*," Grady said to him. *That quick, forgot Grady was with us.* "You live out here in the open?"

Junior murmured something. She couldn't quite hear.

"You're my dad?" she asked, through the fog in her head. Then, she thought of something to test him. "Hey, do you have a brother?"

"I have two so-called brothers, Sam and Buford. Yeah, I'm your dad." He laughed his quick, nervous laugh. "Pretty down on my luck."

"Are you — all right?" she asked.

"I've been worse," he said. "But you're not all right, Buhlly-Buhlly, that's what I called you. Buhlaire." *Buhlaire! My dad, saying my name!* He made her walk faster, and she knew to keep still until they got to where he was taking them.

My dad . . . cares. My dad? Can't believe it. "I've been looking for you," she murmured. "Never thought to look out here," she told him.

"We can talk about it," he said. He laughed again, a kind of country sound all at once. Abruptly, he cut it off. He stood there in place a moment.

Buhlaire sensed something hard, tough, down under the soft part of his voice. She tried to figure out what it was, but she was half-dead on her feet.

They moved steadily along. It was as if she were walking in her sleep. Then they got out of it. She couldn't feel her feet. They half-dragged her.

She found her dad had taken them inside somewhere. She had to blink many times. The blinding light they'd come out of made the sunless inside place seem very dark for a few minutes. Then her eyes adjusted to what was like dusk of evening.

They had walked well within, into a corner of the place. Her dad was very busy doing things. He built up a fire and sat her down in a broken, torn chair beside it. Grady crouched down on the floor. There was a folding bed with a sleeping bag open on it. There was a pillow.

"What is this place?" she asked him.

"An underpass," her dad said. "Outside, above us, are abandoned railroad tracks."

"It's big," she said, looking around. "Like a cave." She didn't feel so good now. She saw other beds, over in the distance. She didn't look for people.

"It echoes," said Grady.

Her dad laughed his odd sound. "Everything's abandoned through here, since the interstate. Lots of left-over people, too."

Carefully, he eased her boots off. She kept her shoes on.

"Can't move my feet," she said.

"Try wiggling your toes," her dad said.

"It hurts!" she cried, moving them a little.

"Good! Pain means your feet haven't froze." He pulled off her gloves and placed them atop the boots, which he put next to the fire. He took her hands between his own. It surprised her, the cool touch of his pale hands. Then, he rubbed hers very fast between his palms.

His hands, stubby-thick and gray, ashy with cold. She could feel tremors through them. His eyes were bright, looking gravely at her.

Living out here, away from the streets, neighborhoods. A left-over man. No. A bum. No. My dad. Homeless. Word. The truth made her ache; it brought a sob to her throat. She covered it by coughing. Her dad let her hands go then. He got up, found a blanket in a heap of stuff near a wall. Clothing and bedding all mixed together, a big, dark pile of it.

Snakes, in there? Nearby, there was a large brown plastic bag full of refuse, cartons, empty cans. Garbage. The place smelled damp, with the dank odor of spoiled food.

"You can put this around you," he said, bringing her an old wool thing. She didn't want to, but she put it around herself. He had leaned down toward her, and she got a whiff of him. He needed a bath.

He sat down beside her, cross-legged.

"So," he said, looking at her. "Hi," he said, smiling boldly. "I'm Theodore Sims. But nobody ever called me Theodore around here. I'm Junior. I'm your dad, I already told you."

"Hi," she murmured back. So weird, him, having held and rubbed her hands. She felt shy. She felt sorry for him, a little ashamed of him. She felt guilty for being ashamed. But her dad, homeless! "I'm Buhlaire-Marie Sims." *I'm your daughter. The Water House child.* She couldn't say daughter to him, where Grady Terrell could hear her. But she and her dad smiled together. Suddenly, he laughed high and loud, startling her. The dim place echoed with his voice.

"Your hands feel all right?" he asked, after a moment. That quickly, he changed back to a quiet man.

"They're tingly. Hurt, a little," she managed to say. She looked into the crackling fire. Felt it warm her. "Don't think I've ever been so cold."

Her hands were aching more than she would say.

But the fire was warming her. Her dad had built it in a metal barrel cut lengthwise and placed on its side. Over the top was a screen. The whole thing brought lots of heat. The place was getting cozy.

Buhlaire and Junior stared at one another. Well, she had a hard time keeping her eyes off him. He'd removed his scarf. She could see his hair. It was shoulder length, the color of her own, except it had gray all through it. Rasta hair, just like hers. *How'd it happen, I wear my hair in twists like his? Skin, near-white and pale, but slightly unclean-looking.*

Buhlaire stared at him, Junior Sims. Couldn't get enough of looking at him. *At last. My dad!* She glanced around at Grady, who kneeled a little ways from them, so they could be more private. She'd not seen Grady at rest, so to speak, when he wasn't knocking into something or trying to beat somebody at something.

She and Grady had their feet close to the fire. Steam came up from the soles of their wet shoes.

Junior moved Buhlaire's boots back from the fire. "They'll melt, rubber," her dad said. He laughed that short sound again.

My dad! She grew quiet, speechless. But there were things she could see about him. He had the look of someone used to not eating all the time. A little weak, hungry-looking. There was lots she would just not think about because he was her dad.

She tucked the blanket in around her legs. Her shivers were stopping. "I was almost frozen," she thought to say. "I can feel the fire real good now."

In a little while she put her warmed, dry boots back on.

They sat there in another quiet between them, when her dad said, "You all in school together?" Glanced over at Grady.

Buhlaire nodded at the fire. She gave a quick look to her schoolmate; then, looked away.

"Why come he follows you?" her dad wanted to know.

Grinning, shaking her head, Buhlaire played with her hands.

"Oh," her dad said, catching on. He laughed his weird laugh. He looked hard at Grady a moment. "That's what you do, follow a girl, 'stead of talking to her? Go call her on the phone, then. But don't go follow her," her dad told him.

"Well, you follow her," Grady said.

"I'm her dad, fella," her dad said, with a threat in his voice.

"I know who you are," Grady said. He got up and backed away. He didn't take his eyes off her dad.

What does he mean? Sounding like he doesn't like my dad. Buhlaire was shocked when her dad got up, went quickly over to Grady.

Tall, but stoop shoulders, looking scary and ragged. . . . Oh! I bet if the coffee shop saw you open the door, they'd call the cops.

Her dad and Grady stood facing each other, menace between them. Her dad: "You follow her — why?" Speaking in a sullen, angry voice.

"So nothing happens to her," Grady answered. "She goes all over the countryside," he said softly.

Buhlaire sat frozen, afraid to breathe, for fear she'd miss a word.

"And what else?" her dad said, peering at Grady. But if there was more, Grady wasn't going to say. He stared down at his feet.

Quiet all around. Her dad said, "Knew I'd seen you before. Now I remember where."

Grady nodded, looked at her dad. "I remember you, too."

"Just don't say anything about it." She thought that's what her dad said to Grady in a real soft voice. "Bad enough she catches me like this, all down on my luck."

Grady cleared his throat. "Yeah." Then, he kept quiet.

"You see that she gets into town when we finish here. Storm'll be passed by then."

"Okay," Grady said.

"Stay back some, it's pretty warm enough in here now," her dad told him.

"Okay," Grady answered again. He stayed back in the shadows as her dad came bounding to the fire. He grinned at Buhlaire. Again, he took her hands in his.

"I'm glad to see you, Buhlly-Buhlly. You remember I always called you that?"

No! No! "Uh-uh," she said shyly.

"But I been wanting to see you for so long. See, I figured you came out here looking for me." He laughed, stared at the fire. "I — I didn't much want you to see me like this."

"Never even knew you were out here. I'd of come looking if I'd known." Somehow, he had made her feel guilty. "Sorry," she murmured.

"Oh, well," he said. He grinned at her and squeezed her hands in his. "I'm glad to see you, anyway. Been wanting to. But I didn't want to come see you, so down on my luck."

He was like some kind of weather that was alive. The way his mood changed in an instant made her anxious. One minute, he was like a long-lost dad. The next, she didn't know what. He surrounded her so that she forgot all about Grady. Her dad's eyes looked bright and sleepy at the same time. Kind of bloodshot and strained, though. But he had the deep, burning eyes that drew her in.

"I just wanted to see you so much," she managed to say.

"Well, now you got me!" he said. He gave her a big hug and laughed, full of glee. She tried to laugh back. But the odor of him — smelly man, her dad — took her breath. *Whew!* Ever so gently, she pushed him away.

9

Back Time

I missed you. "Nobody told me . . . where you were," is what she said. She didn't want him to think she didn't like him, pushing him away like that. She wanted so much to ask him where he'd been her whole life. *That'ud sound too bold.* It might've embarrassed him. Then, she had this hunch, and she connected it to him. All the time, forever, she had these daydreams. They were always there, floating around in her head. No words to them, so she never paid much attention to them. They were like worn-out fluttery curtains, or old flowery wallpaper. And so familiar, she saw them, knew them, but never really *noticed* them. Now, she did, and pinned it on her dad.

A ball . . . A man. I'm on the grass, I see the ball coming. I see sunlight and the man, smiling. My own show. Just always there, like a wish. Wow! It's my own back time! Me and my dad, playing.

Her dad grinned at her. Yet, he was silent.

"You used to play ball with me, didn't you?" she asked shyly. Secretly, she was excited. She knew the daydream was true.

Her dad's face went blank. Then, he looked like a spotlight went on inside him. His face lit up. "Never thought to Gawd you'd remember somethin' like that," he said. He laughed loudly, slapping his thigh. "Almost forgot, myself. Man! Yeah! We sure did, played ball. Play ball! Every day! I swore you'd be a ball player, if you'da been a boy. Too bad . . ."

Her heart sank, aching. She squirmed under her skin. "Sorry," she whispered.

"No, now listen," he told her. "We need young women in the world, too."

She looked away, felt small under his gaze. He upset her with his rough edges, the way he talked to her.

In a man's strong voice, he said, "I meant only, too bad I wasn't . . . we didn't play . . . longer. . . ." Changing from one kind to another before her eyes.

They'd been sitting together for some time, and she still didn't have the courage to ask him where he'd been. But bit by bit, she got an idea of how scattered he was.

"You know, you know, you know?" he said, all of a sudden. Spoken in a singsong, broken-record way. "Er-rum-uh, er-rum-uh." Repeating like that appeared to relax him. Yet, every other moment, he acted different, became strange. He seemed so odd to her.

"You know, you know, Bluezy, I married her because she wanted me to," he said, boasting, sounding like he was just out of high school and still carefree. "Well, well, well." He looked sad. "She didn't have to go get a divorce." And, changing the subject, "You know, you all made some *good* music the other night! You know?"

I knew it was you at Delmore's, your band . . .

"But she had to go make how a married man must settle down," he said, "stay home first. Get my education, so, for a good job." His voice was dark with mocking anger. "But no good job come my way. Huh. Bluezy says you got to, got-to-got-to have the get-up-and-go to get the job, you know. You know. Say I'm sorry for myself. Huh! Huh!" Resentful, "Made me feel all bad inside. But neither of us homebodies, you know-you know. Why come her going somewhere, all time working was all right — you know? And, you know, me going someplace wasn't?"

Out of her jumbled thoughts, Buhlaire said, "Where did you work?" And her dad threw a fit at her.

"Now that's it! That takes the candy!" he yelled at her. "All time starting. Don't you start up. That's it, that takes the sweet from the cake!" He jumped to his feet, trembling all over. His mouth turned down in a sad, clown face. Tears sprang to his eyes.

What is it? What did I do? Buhlaire leaned away from him.

Looking like a hurt child, he began sputtering and slobbering.

She got up, sure she'd done something wrong. She did love him so. She lifted a hand to comfort him, but something held her back. She was scared of him, of touching him, afraid of the sudden swings of his mind. She didn't take her eyes off him.

Her dad lurched like a crazy man, waving his arms and crying like a baby. He went over and fell on his cot hard enough to break it, put an old couch pillow over his head. Softly, he was sobbing. She could see his shoulders shake.

Buhlaire felt numb. She didn't know what to do or what to say. Now, beyond his bed, she could see others. A few people on the far side in the shadows. People, coming in where it was warm. Instantly, she was alert to them, ready to protect herself. These were real down people. No telling what they might do, she thought.

Way over there against the wall, one of them sat himself on the couch, stretched out. Another was looking, watching. She grew aware of someone standing in that cool space beyond her dad's bed. Someone, with hands on hips, peered over at her. Someone was watching her.

It made her freeze inside. Someone, inching around her dad, wary of him. Someone was in the light and shadow, someone cautiously coming closer to the open.

"Buhlaire!" Whispering, it was Grady.

Grady! She'd forgotten him again. Now, she felt so relieved he was still there.

He motioned her over where he was, but she couldn't move. She shook her head. He waved at her, pointing the way out. She should go with him, get out of there. He was afraid of all the people. More coming in now, on the far side, like bats coming home to the cave. *Vampires!* As if they'd been feeding outside and now were coming back into this — *this other where! Another world.* Still, Buhlaire couldn't make herself leave.

My dad. My poor dad. She wrung her hands, struggled with herself, feeling all unsure. *Why'd I have to go say something! What did I say?*

Suddenly, her dad sat up on the side of the bed. He sat primly with his feet together and his hands folded in his lap. What did he look like, sitting like that, so alone? *In this place. In this awful cold place!* Not who, but what. She couldn't think what him sitting like that reminded her of. She had no time.

Swiftly, he wiped his face on his sleeve; then, returned to that straight position. At last, he looked over at her. He looked to be half smiling at her. It was then she thought to go over to him. Her fear had settled into the steady pounding of her heart.

Before she could move, she saw someone about to creep by his bed. Someone, walking so slowly, it was like he — she, it was a she — thought maybe he wouldn't notice her.

Her dad hissed. "No, you don't," he told the person. "You stay away from my kid!" He stumbled to his feet.

"That your kid? That who she is, your daughter?" A woman, ageless, maybe fifty. Hard to tell, she was so bundled in raggedy clothes.

"Don't you even think about it!" he hissed at

her. He swept his arm out and across, as though he meant to sweep her out of his sight. If the woman came forward, she would surely run into his sweeping arm.

"I said, get on back where you belong," her dad warned the woman.

"Is that any way to talk to your mother?" the woman asked. "I ain't going to hurt that child. She's my grandbaby!"

"No she's not!" he shouted at the woman. Frantic, he told Buhlaire, "She's *not* my mother! She's a crazy, a crazy woman!"

The woman meant to smile sweetly at Buhlaire, squinting her eyes, pouring it on. "I had a boy," she purred. "A sweet child, just like you. But then, I lost him. But now he's a man. But that's all right, long as I found him. . . ."

Her dad kept sweeping his arm out, and the woman kept coming on. It was clear to Buhlaire that her dad didn't want to hit the woman. He backed up toward Buhlaire while he kept swinging, and the woman kept coming on.

"Let's get out of here," Grady whispered. He put his hand on her arm, as if to lead her away. She shook it off.

"I can't leave my dad like this," she murmured to him.

"But, Buhlaire!"

She ignored him, shook him off again. She kept her eyes on her dad and the woman.

The woman sat on her knees on the floor. Junior

Sims bent down to speak. "You do one more thing," he said, "and you'll be ten times more than sorry."

"Doesn't make any difference," the woman said, "I'm still your — "

" — Shut! Don't say it. It's a lie! Buhlly-Buhlly? You know. I don't have a mom. You know?"

The woman cackled. She hugged herself, rocking and crowing with delight. "The man is sooo funny! Nobody born without a mom."

"I know what I'm saying," he said stubbornly. "Far as I'm concerned, I was just born with — nobody."

One of his — vanilla.

It's his mind, Buhlaire thought. It's off the track.

"But I'm your mom come back," the woman told her dad.

"No'm," he said. "Uh-uh."

"How you know I'm not? I could be, probably am," she said.

"Because I know," Buhlaire's dad said. "The way Buhlly-Buhlly knows I'm her dad. She don't remember, I used to hold her when she cried." His voice caught; his hands shook. He went on anyway. "She knows me because it's the kind of thing you just know.

"See?" he said to Buhlaire. "When I was a kid, once in a while I'd run into other kids I just knew came from the same place I did — the county home. You know, is all. And it's something you grow up knowing."

All the time he spoke, there was a shifty look in

his eyes. Made Buhlaire not quite believe he was an orphan. Like he'd made it up. She thought so.

He turned to the woman. "And no way do you belong to me," he told her. He turned his back on her.

Buhlaire said to him, "I knew right away you were who you said you were. My dad." She looked up at him, cared for him so much.

While the woman had been talking, Buhlaire had come right up to her dad, as though she meant to protect him. He took her hand once again, and they held hands a moment. It seemed to her the most natural thing between them. His hand was warm now, with tiny tremors. She didn't mind them. She smiled at him. Placed her head on his chest for a moment. It was hard for her, but she could stand the way he was. And ever so gently, he touched her Rasta hair. *Fingers like butterflies.*

Her dad led her the few steps over to where they had been seated before.

The fire he'd made was now a hot furnace of burning coals. All around the fire barrel for a few feet, it felt like summertime, and all around the underpass there were other fire barrels now. The fires made Buhlaire think of bright heat blossoms. Yet she knew the cold was just beyond them, right where that woman sat watching and listening.

"Pay her no mind," he told Buhlaire. "I guess she's got nothing else to do with herself."

"I think she must be lonely," Buhlaire said.

"Yeah, well," he said glumly. Suddenly, his mood

shifted. "Okay! Great! I'm glad we got this chance to talk and stuff. Wow!" His eyes gleamed at her.

Fresh breeze through the screen. He changes that quick.

He lowered his head, wouldn't look at her. "Sorry you had to see me like this," he said.

"But I'm . . . I'm just so . . . glad you're here!" she said. She didn't know what else to say.

"No, I know how I must look. I'm . . . I'm so down on my luck," he told her. "I'd be okay, though, if I just had a little stake — "

"I can get you one," she said. "I mean, the coffee shop has all kinds of sandwiches." She was happy she could do something to help him.

"Oh, lord, hee, hee!" went the woman who wouldn't go away.

"No. No, I don't mean food," her dad said. "Look, Buhlly-Buhlly, all I need is to get on my feet." Nervously, he scratched through his hair.

To Buhlaire, it sounded like scraping on sandpaper.

"Uhmm," he said, "you want some soup?"

Mind, jumping like he can't keep it in one place. Without a pause, he'd gone somewhere else.

"I got some soup somewhere," he went on. "Yeah. That'd be a good idea."

"You want me to fix it?" Buhlaire asked, eager to please him.

"Yeah! Yeah! We'll have some of my soup. Over in the pile, I got goods and stuff. Good-making soup."

Buhlaire sighed, and followed as he went over

there. The woman was right behind them. Her dad had given up trying to get rid of the person. He looked right through the woman as he walked around her.

"He's got all kinds of stuff in that pile," the woman said to Buhlaire. She scurried near, but not too close. "Afraid somebody's going to take some food if he don't bury it on his 'hilltop.' " She kept her distance. Buhlaire was glad of that.

The woman went on. "Probably true they'd take it. Folks is all the time hungry. Oh, and they call me Peggy. You must be Buhlly-Buhlly. I didn't recognize you at first, you've grown so."

Buhlaire was startled. But she didn't trust the woman. Didn't believe she knew her before. *She could've heard my dad call me Buhlly-Buhlly.*

Her dad pulled something from the pile. He brought out several things. The woman, Peggy, was right there, close enough that her dad knew she was there.

"Here," he said to Peggy. "Give 'em to her." He handed an armful of articles to the woman. Gingerly, Peggy clutched all of it close. She brought it over to Buhlaire.

It wasn't food that her dad had handed to Peggy. Buhlaire sank to her knees as Peggy set the armful on the floor.

Now Buhlaire saw that her dad had found a couple of cans of soup, and the woman went to the fire with them. She heard scraping. She could hear Peggy coming and going, but she didn't look around again to see.

What was on her mind was the stuff her dad had uncovered and Peggy had handed to her. She stared at it on the floor before her. Seeing it knocked her brain wide open. Made her insides feel all shaky. Then, she pulled at one thing, and another, arranging them one by one, like missing cards from a deck.

It must be! All his hair cut real short. My dad! And me, I'm so little. I know that's me. My dad is holding me!

Grady leaned over her. Cautiously, he looked all around before kneeling beside her. "Buhlaire? What's all this stuff?" he asked her.

"It's . . . it's about me. Look. Medals I got for basketball. Just last year! And two in the shape of this state, one in silver and one in gold, for music — Chorus. It was a county and a regional competition. You know how you forget things like that? A year's a long time. I lose things, too, and have to be reminded. Was it just last year? But we got these medals for getting rated Superior and Merit. I didn't realize they were missing. I forgot them — it's the way I am. *Am I strange?*"

"You are way other," Grady said, only half joking. He touched one of the pictures. "That little girl is you?" he asked.

"Oh, a long time ago, I think," she answered. "And look at my dad." She picked out a snapshot of him. "He doesn't have Rasta hair yet. And Mom! It's our family. And look at this one."

She found a small photograph of her mother holding a hose and drinking from it. *Snap!* "Mom doesn't look like Bluezy at all." Her mom in cutoff jeans and a T-shirt. The Montgomery Falls River, all sparkly, was behind her back. There were other pictures, things in a soiled manilla envelope.

There's probably more stuff, too. Buhlaire glanced over at the mound of clothing. It was a dark, jumbled mess, piled high. *What all is in there? Did he "take" stuff about me? Aunt Digna! My dad, a thief! She thinks so.* Buhlaire didn't care to go further with the idea of stolen goods. But what she thought next made her sad. *He took my things. He took off with my back time. He sure did. Maybe he just wanted to have me with him. That's why he took the stuff! It would be like having me pay attention to him!* Buhlaire sucked air in, held her breath a moment at the thought. *Attention must be paid. Him, missing me, just like I'm missing him.* It was all too much. She didn't know whether to feel good, or bad.

"What?" Grady asked, watching her closely.

She shook her head and began putting things into the manilla envelope. Pictures went in first, then the medals, which she carefully placed at the bottom.

"We need to leave," Grady said. There was noise. It echoed in waves off the concrete walls. Grady looked all around them.

Buhlaire didn't say anything. She got up, took the bookbag from her shoulder and put her arms through the straps so it rested on her back. All the time, her dad and the woman, Peggy, had been watching and waiting for her. She clutched the envelope to her chest and went over there.

"I could've done that," Buhlaire said to Peggy. The soup was steaming in a dark pot, already made. "Where did you get water?"

"Clean snow!" Peggy looked at her as if she were stupid. Then she grinned. "Wasn't nothing to do," she said. "Let's get busy!" She laughed, "Hee-hee-hee!"

"Sit on down," her dad told Buhlaire, and she obeyed at once. They ate out of hot–cold cups. There were no spoons. Buhlaire and Grady had to blow on the soup for a good while before they could slurp it down. It was tomato soup. She tried not to notice that the cups had been used.

Peggy was with them. She sat next to Grady while Buhlaire and her dad talked quietly. Again, her dad was caring, a little distant, but still, like her father, and no stranger.

"Soup makes you feel warm inside," he said, as a matter of fact.

She didn't have to answer. They grinned at one another when her stomach growled. She didn't know how hungry she'd become.

"Must be lunchtime," she said. "Tomato soup is my favorite."

"Mine, too," he said. His eyes were bright, looking at her. Then, he was lost in thought a moment before he said, "I see you got it all in the envelope. There's more. I can give you some more sometime.

See, I took some things when I — when Bluezy and I parted our ways. . . ."

She listened. His eyes sparkled at her. "I'd come back to see you," he said softly. She leaned close, barely able to hear him. It was like he'd gone inside himself. "Wasn't s'pose to come near you. I . . . I had my troubles. They . . . they had a right to worry how it might bother you, seeing me . . . uh . . . I wasn't in control . . . worse than now."

"When . . . was the last time you came to see me?" She held her breath, hoping she wouldn't upset him. She knew it must've been not too long ago. But she did upset him with the question. She could tell.

He looked off. Looked angry. Shook his head, saying, "Sometimes, nobody'd be home. If Digna was gone, Babe would let me in. I had a right to you! Sam, like some po-lice man. I wasn't going to hurt you!"

He shook all over, as if he were cold. After a while, the shaking seemed to lessen. It didn't stop, but she could ignore it now.

Her longing bubbled out of her in a stream: "Dad, we could find a place to live. Lots of kids live with just their dads."

He looked slyly at her, then away; and took her by surprise when he said, "Like, a stake won't be the kind you eat." His voice was low and gritty. "You furnish me with some 'stash,' you dig? Like something to keep me going so's I can pull myself up? I don't mean nothing like a bus ticket. If I had me some stash, I could get my *own* bus ticket. I mean, *we*. But what *we* need is to get started, to . . . get my *mind* straight again — you know? You know?" He didn't wait for her reply. "Need to get myself cleaned up — how much stash you got?" The last part rolled off his tongue so fast and low, she almost missed it.

Finally, she understood. But what he wanted from her had been hard work. It hadn't been so easy for her to come by. *Oh, Dad. I love you, Daddy*. "I've got some," she said. "I've got the money for us to start."

10

Grady

"See? He breaks in your own house and takes what's not his. He could've been in there last week for all you know." Grady talked fast as they hurried away.

"Aunt Babe would let him in," Buhlaire told him. "He came by to see me, and I wasn't home." *He'd come in the early day when everybody was busy working somewhere. Uncle Sam.* "Anyway, is it any of your business, too?" Buhlaire didn't say that as harshly as she might've. But it shut him up so she could think. Everything was moving along. The feeling for her dad spilled over into the air to Grady.

They were on their way back toward town. The whole day, too, had turned around. *Just upside down!* When they came out from the underpass, they found the sky was blue and endless. *Cold everywhere. But it can't touch me! Me and my dad. Going away with him!*

There was a slight warmth to the sun on her face. Snow on the ground glistened with a sheen of melt on top. It was as if the snowstorm and the terrible whiteout had never been. There were even places where wind had swept the ground flat-out smooth, cleaned of snow.

Buhlaire's brain was just as clear. She stopped still where she was, clutching the envelope to her. Her hands were warm fists inside her gloves. "You know something?" she said to Grady. "Get this. This is the first time you ever been talking to me straight up. And now you are all in my face."

"Buhlaire . . ."

"No, no, bwoy. I mean, I know who you are. I just don't know who you think you are." She stuck her nose up in the air and started on again.

Grady was behind her. In a minute he was almost at her side. She gave him a hard glance. He gave her more space.

"Well, in there," he began. "In that underpass — a *cave* — I thought everything was changed. And in the whiteout . . ." He sounded a little shy toward her.

She humpfed at him. But she remembered, when the whiteout hit, she'd called for him. She'd trusted him to save her. He would've, too, she supposed, if not for her dad. Her dad saved both of them. *Things have changed, all right. You're right about that.*

Her dad, she thought, and felt really good inside. *I can help him, I don't mind. We take the money, and we're gone!*

"I know how you feel about him," Grady said. "I got a dad, too."

She'd not thought about him having a dad or mom. Uncle Sam, too, was one like that, someone who was good at being alone. She was like that, too.

"Do I know your dad?"

"You'd recognize him if you saw him," Grady said. "You might not know he's my dad." He changed the subject to her: "Everybody says you're stuck-up with your head in the clouds."

That hurt her. "I couldn't care less about your idiot friends."

"Don't get so mad all the time," he said. "We're just talking."

Well, she knew they were, and she was glad. *I mean, we went in to my dad's separate. We come out to walk together. He's talking to me like I'm somebody's friend. His.* That almost pleased her. But her dad was there everywhere on her mind. All the excitement was so light inside her. It kept rising, lighter and lighter. It felt as light as air. But maybe it was wearing thin. *If I go with him, where do we go? Do I have to sleep outside? No, the money. We can find someplace. . . .*

"Look, I knew your dad before," Grady said.

"Before — what?" she asked. She kept walking, her head still up. How did he know her dad? she wondered. She wasn't sure what she should do, where she should go. How could she go home? *Have to get to the bank sometime.*

"I knew your dad from the shelter," Grady told her.

She slowed, looking at him. "What are you talking about? The Shelter From *Any* Storm?"

"I lived there once. I've seen your dad there."

"You're saying — you mean you . . ."

". . . I mean me and my dad. When I was six.

We didn't have anything after he lost his job. But he had me, and I had him. And so the shelter took us in. It wasn't as nice as it is now."

Once he got started, Grady told her all he could. "But my dad, if he had but a stone and a nail, he could fix something with them. Better'n that, he could take care of people."

Grady smiled at the ground. "We lived in an old bus once, with some others. He'd go out and get stuff before anybody else besides me was awake. Always made me go with him, too. That was before my aunt and uncle lived around here. Never left me alone with anybody. Said, 'Whatever happens, it's going to happen to us both together.'

"We had a room once, but then we couldn't pay and had to skip out at night. My dad hated doing that. He always said he'd pay the people back, and he did. Sent them the money when he got on his feet."

"Is he on his feet? I mean . . . you live in a house, right?"

"Yeah, sure!" Grady said. They had stopped on their way. "We can rent a house now. Rent, someday to buy it, too."

Buhlaire felt she couldn't stand up another minute. She sank to her knees. Grady kneeled beside her. "You all right?" he asked.

She grinned. "Have to find a rest room. But I can wait," she said. "I want to hear all about it. My dad?"

"See, the shelter took him in, too. Your dad gets

cleaned up there sometimes. He'll not stay more than a day and a night."

Then, Grady went on about his dad. "See, my dad knew how to take care of people. He fit right in with the works of the shelter. We first got there, he volunteered. He helped anybody. Made beds. He did everything with one arm around me. He did! He did!"

Buhlaire searched his eyes, stunned by the picture.

"Wherever he went, I went with him," Grady said. "With his arm always around me. I mean, he could be serving food on the line. He'd have the soup ladle in one hand, and the other arm around me. If he was standing talking to some guys, he'd turn me into his chest and have both arms around me as he talked. I was little, but my legs were gettin' long!"

"My gosh!" Buhlaire murmured. She shook her head from side to side in astonishment. But, really, she wanted to hear about her own dad. Yet, it was interesting, what he was telling her.

"I always remember that," Grady said. "See, I was mad all the time, though, even if my dad did have his arm around me. I wanted my mom. I remember her shape. Then the shape just wasn't there anymore."

Buhlaire got to her feet. The picture of his mom made her cry. It came out sounding like the cry of a little kid who'd fallen and scraped both knees and an elbow.

He reached out his hand, barely touched her. "Oh, man!"

Her crying out stopped almost as soon as it started. It was like a sudden storm that came quickly and went soon. She got hold of herself. "I have to go someplace, and I don't know where. I got a home, but I don't want to go to it. I hate all of them! They hate my dad! I don't know what to do." *I want to be with my dad!* Yelling it inside.

"Your mom, Bluezy Sims, not home?"

"No," she sighed, sniffling a little. "Not so you could notice it. It's me and Aunt Digna and Aunt Babe. Aunt Babe's blind."

"Like to meet all them sometime," he said. "You never see them around."

She didn't want to share her relatives with him right now. "You go to the A.M.E. church?"

"No," he said. "Why?"

"Neither do I," she said. "But you could meet them there. They sometimes go, when Aunt Babe's up to it. But I don't know. Anymore, my aunts don't seem to get along too well. Everything's breaking down, I guess."

"Shoot," he said. "It's the winter. It's the cold. It'll get warm one of these days. Things get good when it's warm."

"I — hope so," she said. *I'll be long gone from here by then.*

"Buhlaire."

"We'd better go on," she said. "Ooh, I don't know where to go," she said, sobbing again.

"Listen. Come on with me. We'll go to the shelter. My dad *runs* it now."

"You are kidding me!"

"There's a director, but my dad does the day-to-day managing of everything," Grady said. "And nothing, nobody, stays there without him knowing about it."

"Wow!" she said. "That's a big place to run."

"Well, there's people working all kinds-a jobs," Grady told her. "Food people, servers, cooks. Maintenance. Guards. Office workers and stuff. Lots of volunteers working for food and small change. I don't know what all. I work my own hours. I keep track of food donations along with this man, Mr. Contell. We use leftovers for soups. We get free stuff from all over the place. Come on with me. You don't have to stay all night. But you could if you wanted to."

"I have to go to the bank."

"Buhlaire."

"Huh?"

"I know it's none of my business. But don't give him your money."

"You shut up about my dad!"

"Sorry," he mumbled.

"I don't need you. I don't have to go to anybody's shelter." She felt cold saying that, but she couldn't stop herself. "I can walk around all night if I have to, and nobody can stop me. I can go live with my dad!" *In a cave?* Buhlaire squeezed her eyes closed to blot out the image of the underpass.

"I . . . I didn't mean nothing by it," Grady said. "It's just — "

"Just nothing!" she said. "It's not your business."

"Look, I went with you to your dad's. Can't you come meet my dad? He's a nice guy. I want him to meet you, too. Please? We got public rest rooms. . . ." He grinned at her and looked shy all of a sudden.

Two good reasons for her to go on over with him. Plus, she wanted to. He'd gone in the underpass with her, and he did what her dad asked by walking back with her. Plus, she had to use the facilities.

"Well, all right," she said. "I have to hurry!"

Halfway there, she looked at him and said, "You sure act like a different person out of school!"

"Well, so do you, too," he said. Then, "We can go in the kitchen at the shelter. Get some good hot chocolate."

"I like hot chocolate when it's cold outside," she said, walking fast beside him.

"You never want it when it's warm out," he agreed.

"That's for sure."

Later on, in town, but before they got to the shelter, Buhlaire had to tell him something.

"Grady. Back there? When I . . . I cried . . ."

"It wasn't nothing. I've seen girls cry before. I can cry," he said.

"It was because what you said is just how I feel,"

she said. "Like, whenever I wake up and my mom's gone again."

He was quiet for a time. Just before they turned the corner to the shelter, he said, "My dad says he'll tell me what happened to her. Someday. But not to worry. My mom's alive."

My dad's alive. There was nothing more to say. They went inside the building. He showed her where the rest rooms were.

Afterward, he was waiting in the corridor. Behind him, she could see into a long dormitory room. Women and children. It seemed wrong to stare at them.

Buhlaire dragged her feet, she was so tired. She felt low one minute, and about to burst with happiness the next.

They ran into his dad coming out of an office area. He gave one swift look at Buhlaire. He caught his son in a gentle headlock and pulled him down the hall. "What'er you doin' home at lunchtime? I'll put you to work." He turned all the way around with Grady so he could say something to Buhlaire. Grady was laughing and saying, "Dad, quit it, quit it!" and trying to pull his dad's strong arm away from his neck and shoulders.

"Come on," Mr. Terrell told her. "There's some lunch right down this way."

She grinned at him. "We already had some soup," she said. He didn't seem angry at them for being there when they should've been at school. *He's nice.*

"Guess who . . . she is," Grady managed to say

as his father held him sideways in the headlock all the way to the kitchen.

"Know who she is," said his dad. "Everybody knows Bluezy's daughter." He was kind of gruff. He didn't smile, or not smile. He was ordinary-looking. His eyes got big and wide at her, as if he were playing with her, but accepting of who she was.

His saying that everybody knew her surprised and pleased her. *I didn't know that. Someday, everybody's gonna know me by my first name, too.*

She would remember this day as the one when she made a friend out of an enemy. Grady. And the day her dad saved her. She would remember it as the day she felt she belonged somewhere. Funny that it would be the Shelter From *Any* Storm that made her feel at home. *Not some home. Not even some cave.* "I'm Buhlaire," she told Grady's dad. "Buhlaire-Marie Sims is my full name."

"Proud," Mr. Terrell said, and nodded at her. The word hung there on thin air, like some award he'd presented to her.

Means he's proud to meet me — man!

Lunchtime, and the kitchen was in an uproar. "You two sit over there by the window. Chicago will get to you in a minute. I have to go back out in the hall." His father left them. Buhlaire was sorry he couldn't sit down with her and Grady. She liked the way being close to him made you feel sort of good. But who was Chicago?

"Dad'll be back in a little while," Grady told her. He led her over to a long white table, out of the way but in front of a tall window. The table was smooth on top, but with dark showing where it had chipped along the sides. They could see the whole large kitchen and everybody working. She'd never sat down in an eating place quite so big, except for their lunchroom at school.

Out the window, Buhlaire could see down into a courtyard where children were sitting on walls they'd made from snow.

Noise was all around her, people hurrying in and out of the kitchen. People were doing their jobs as quickly as possible. Some guys carried huge pots of soup and other stuff, like stew, onto a cart with wheels. Then they wheeled the food out of the kitchen and down toward the hall where she had been the first time.

Some big guys and a woman were at work tables making sandwiches, and at the stoves. People shouted, joked back and forth around the big kitchen. Others didn't say anything. But all of them were moving, doing something. Stacks of sandwiches were put on large trays and carried out.

"Some volunteers first came to find shelter just like me and my dad did," Grady told her. "Lot of folks feel better about having free food and a free bed when they get to help out."

Help your sister, brother, human. The kitchen was all silvery. Everything in it that was kitchen looked to be stainless steel. Except for the table where she and Grady sat. It had to be the table where the staff ate. All else, sinks, counters, long work tables, refrigerator units, were made of steel. "Everything gleams at you," she said. The stoves were big and dark silver, big and heavy.

"People made donations for this kitchen. Businesses."

Someone slid two brown mugs of hot chocolate across the table at them.

Grady caught them. "Man, be careful!" he said to the big man who brought them over.

"Hush up 'fore I finish your head."

"You, simple," Grady said, then ducked as the big man pretended to come over and get him.

Buhlaire grinned into her cup and took her gloves off. She tasted the sweet chocolate. It was the world's best. *No 'bout a doubt it!* Somebody slid a plate of cupcakes with white icing across the table. *Mercy!*

"Save me," Buhlaire said softly. She reached for a cupcake.

"Chicago made the hot chocolate," Grady said.

"It is the best!" Buhlaire said.

"Chicago, she says your chocolate's the best," Grady called out.

"Thank you, thank you," said the big man who had brought it to them, not turning from his work. He was at the sink, washing pans that had been on the stove. A great cloud of hot-water steam rose up around him.

Chicago was one of the three kitchen bosses, Grady told her. He had a blue bandanna covering his bald head and a black one around his neck. Otherwise, he wore a white undershirt, sweated through, as if it were spring. He wore clean white pants and rubber boots. He had a helper, a young man about high school age. He gave the sink work over to the young man.

"Cupcake didn't waste no time on your plate," another man said. He leaned on the table between her and Grady.

Buhlaire suddenly realized he was talking to her.

"What about my cupcake?" the man said, bluntly, and waited for an answer.

Buhlaire swallowed, and boldly asked, "Can I have another?"

"That's better, pretty child." He didn't smile.

"That's Keno," Grady told her.

Keno put a large metal tray full of cupcakes with chocolate icing into the hands of a helper, who took them out to the hall.

Grady told her that Keno was second boss of the kitchen. He had white clothes on with a big white apron over them down to his ankles. He was as puny-looking as Chicago was strong. She took another cupcake from the table plate. Keno saw her. "That's right, fatten you up. Looking like a tall, skinny bird."

No I don't! She didn't say it. But she was pleased they were all paying attention to her.

"Man can bake anything," Grady told her.

Matilda Whitlaw was another boss of the kitchen, Grady told Buhlaire. He was talking softly. Matilda

Whitlaw was there, standing in the winter light of a wide window. Buhlaire couldn't see her face because the daylight was behind her back. The woman had been at the stove. But now she stood in a far window, facing them. Almost at once, Buhlaire knew by the way she stood so long, so unmoving, that there was something wrong with her.

"They call her Mizduhbya," Grady said, very quietly. "You know why?"

It took Buhlaire a minute, but then she knew why. She told Grady, "It's Miz for Miss. It's duhbya for the letter W, the first letter of her last name — is that right? Said real fast: Mizduhbya." *People are so funny!* Grady talked low, she realized, so as not to upset Mizduhbya.

"Thinks everybody is always whispering about her," Grady said. "She thinks cars are following her."

It's her mind. Like my dad.

Mr. Terrell was back and sat down with them. Things seemed to get quiet when he was there. Chicago brought him some soup and crackers.

Mr. Terrell ate his soup, and watched her between tablespoonfuls. She liked him, the way she'd suddenly known she liked Grady with just a walk with him. But she felt a little ashamed not having a normal dad herself, and being an outside child. *A Water House child.* Wondered if they knew.

She kept her hand on the manilla envelope. Mr. Terrell saw she did.

Grady said, "Her dad gave her some stuff of hers he had."

She didn't feel she could explain any further than that. Mr. Terrell would know people like her dad. She felt he would.

"We got caught outside of town in a whiteout. Me and Grady," was what she thought to say. And blurted out more, "I've never been so scared in my life." She kept on surprising herself. *Don't know what I'm going to come out with!* She looked at Grady's dad and felt herself smiling.

"Out by the interstate," he said. "People here were talking about it. But I hear it was over quick. Folks out there come into town every few days," he explained to her, about the underpass people. "We go out there with apples and sandwiches."

"And free for them," Grady said proudly.

"My . . . my dad's . . . out there. Junior Sims."

Mr. Terrell nodded. It was easy to tell him things. *Don't even know him.* She felt as if she'd known him a long time.

"We saw him," Grady said.

"We went in there," she said. "They always told me he was dead in Vietnam. But I found him. He's alive! But you know what? I think he's mental . . . ill. That's why he acts strange."

Mr. Terrell was kind. "A whole lot happens to some of us in backwater places like this," he said. "People think not, but it does. I come from around here, too."

"My dad acts . . . funny," she said. She felt relief,

saying it. "He changes and changes real fast."

He smiled with sympathy.

"There's a woman out there says she's his mother. It would make her my grandmother. Name of Peggy," Buhlaire told him.

He shrugged his shoulders to say he didn't know about that. But probably he could tell she'd like to have some back-time grandma.

"All kinds of things happen to people," he told her. "Some are helpless against it."

"I know," she said. "I know he can't help himself, my dad — you'd think they'd know better," she said.

"Who?" Mr. Terrell asked.

"My mom, and my aunts. Uncle Sam."

"I see," he said. He started to say something else, but changed his mind.

They talked together so easily. The conversation flew back and forth. Chicago brought Mr. Terrell coffee. Mr. Terrell drank it, blowing on it. Buhlaire watched him and then Grady, then him again. Something about him pleased her. She told him how her mom was never there. "Makes me feel worthless," she said.

She spoke about her missing dad, that it was Mr. Earl who had told her that her dad was alive. She wondered out loud why her mom and Aunt Digna hadn't talked about him. Had lied about him. And then, just as easily as breathing, she knew why. The reason floated back, as though it had been born to drift in her mind. Aunt Digna saying, *"One of Junior's, vanilla."*

So that's it. Vanilla — is ice cream. Is white. She could tell by Mr. Terrell's expression, he knew, and knew she knew.

"People have their prejudices. Against mixing," he said.

She thanked him in her heart for not saying that her mom, her aunt Digna, were prejudiced against her dad's — well, she didn't know which parent it was Aunt Digna spoke of as vanilla. *But the way she said it!* Again, Buhlaire heard Aunt Digna spitting out the word. As if the sound of it was something really bad.

Made me not want to remember it. Not want to know. She wasn't going to ask Mr. Terrell if her dad's mother was of another race. That way, race couldn't ever matter between her and her dad.

"I think prejudice is truly stupid," she said, all at once. "It . . . it really hurts people." *Hurts so bad!*

He shifted in his chair. "The hardest thing is understanding that our parents aren't perfectly good," he said. "That they make mistakes. They're human. And I don't suppose yours probably should of done you the way they did. Kids understand more than we think."

"But you are doing it to me," Grady said, sounding something like a child. "You are telling me someday, about my mom."

His father covered his mouth. Suddenly, he looked so tired. He nodded at his son, said, "I guess whatever grownups do, they are prone to do it wrong. Maybe there's no right." He half-smiled, sadly, it seemed to Buhlaire.

They stayed quiet a moment, glancing at one another.

"You all skipped school. That's okay. But not tomorrow," Mr. Terrell told Grady.

Then Grady had to go say, "Buhlaire's going to go off with her dad. She has to get to the bank for some money."

Mr. Terrell shook his head. "Don't give him some of your money," he told her.

She stuck out her chin. *Do what I want, too. Why is it everybody's business what I do?*

He got up then, and walked away from them. But a few paces, he turned around, said to her, "Excuse me for minding your business. But if he didn't keep you close once, he won't again." He left them.

Who do you think you are! That's so mean, saying that to me.

"Don't get mad at him, he's only trying to help you," Grady said.

"Just . . . leave me alone," she said back.

"Buhlaire, I hope you don't go off with your dad."

"Thanks for the food." She got up, preparing to leave.

"I'm-a tell your mom," he said, desperate to have her stay.

She grabbed her gloves and the envelope, kicked back the chair. "You can't tell her anything 'cause she does not *exist*! Just like your mom. Maybe they are all the same mom. They don't be anywhere!"

She could feel the whole room watching her as she went out.

"Buhlaire."

Make me sick. She actually felt sick inside.

She didn't look back, either.

By the time she made it to the entrance, her eyes were stinging with angry tears. That's when she saw Mr. Terrell again. He said, "Think about what I told you, Miss." He turned and went off with some people coming in. *Just cold!* She looked around, but Grady was nowhere to be seen. He didn't follow her this time. So she went on to the bank.

The bank didn't give her any trouble. She and Aunt Babe had a savings account. That way, she could withdraw her own money. Together they had more than a thousand dollars. But Buhlaire's share was just under four-hundred dollars. *I'll take out two for me and my dad. If I need more, I can come back.* She'd never take any of Aunt Babe's. She hadn't been nervous, even though she'd never taken out so much at one time. Got it in tens and twenties. Nobody asked her why. But maybe they planned to check later. She got out of there.

Then she headed for home. *Not even going to make up a story. Tell them straight up. To their faces. Word.*

11

Hard Home Ground

City sounds slowly faded as Buhlaire walked through the last daylight and entered the Montgomery Falls River lowland. The sun and clear sky of an hour ago was now filmed over by a grimy, dishwater grayness, ready for the drain. She wrinkled her nose in disgust.

A high-up sky. She supposed it could be a sign of more changing weather. *Maybe some sleet. Snap! But that gray will have to fall, some, first. Not a single snow cloud; only can see that dark, ugly slick up there.*

Buhlaire was back on home ground. Friendly territory. She held the manilla envelope tightly to her chest. And barely noticed she'd entered the winding walkway. The planks were cleared of ice and snow. Such a long walkway, but always shoveled and sprinkled with salt pellets to cause some melting.

She saw an occasional tenant of the Water Houses hurrying along the walkways toward town. Some of the younger kids who belonged out here scurried along. She didn't wave or otherwise pay any attention to anybody.

She was thinking about the gifts her father had

given her. *Where will we go, and how will we live? Me and my dad.* She was thinking about that, like a dream ready to come true. Before she'd left him, he said she should bring him money. He said he thought it'd be okay if she went with him. But he would think about it some more, he said. "*Bublly-Bublly, we are going to get together. Know it! You know it! Things gonna be better once I get myself clean — cleaned up and get me a room.*" She remembered every word he had said only for her to hear.

Now she was thinking about more than one room for them both. Maybe Aunt Babe would give her some of her money. She could pay it back. And she could take the rest of her own money out of the bank.

If he didn't keep you close . . . he won't . . . Words. Grady's dad talking, staying with her on the way home. So did thoughts she would never say to her dad. Things she'd said to him. Her mind was like alphabet soup. Too many voices, too much. She felt all shivery inside and tired out.

Sycamore trees around her were snow-covered and ice-slick now after the storm. The dark bark and limbs shone in places, making light and shadow. She knew she was invisible walking through them. The Water Houses were gone as well.

I'll not look for them. Houses will come see me when I'm ready. She played a game of it. Pretending Water Houses would come back when she bid them come.

Because of the heavy trees, she couldn't see much

down by the river. But she could hear voices. She stopped a moment, listening. She heard singing:

> *"When I've done the best I can,*
> *and my friends don't understand —"*

It's Aunt Babe singing!

> *"Then my Lord will carry me home."*

The church song was one of the most beautiful to Buhlaire. She stood there awhile.

Aunt Digna was down there, too. She heard her voice go, "Babe, why you always have to get so sad? You're the one wanted to come walk down here on the water. Wasn't that how you put it?"

"Then why can't I sing what I want, if it's my show?" Babe answered.

Another voice broke into song:

> *"I want to live the life I sing about, in my song!*
> *I want to live right and always shun wrong."*

Mom!

> *"I want to live the life I sing about, in my song!"*

It was Bluezy. *Mom! At home!*

What was happening down there? Buhlaire wondered. Cautiously, she moved down toward the river. She wanted to run down there. But she also wanted to hear what was going on without being seen. They wouldn't see her in the trees until she was right on them. Where were they, anyway? She kept her feet on the ground, sliding them along in the snow. *I'm cold!* Her bookbag was a cold slab against her.

Buhlaire stood among the first line of trees above the shoreline. She hid behind the trunk of a slender, white-covered shape, where she peeked out to watch.

They stood on the Montgomery Falls ice with their feet planted; all of them in a little circle, holding hands. *Hand-holding!* The big surprise was that Uncle Sam was with them. He held Aunt Babe's hand, and Bluezy's on the other side.

Buhlaire could see them all. Aunt Digna's back was to her and the shore. Digna held Aunt Babe's and Bluezy's other hands.

Holding hands! They think it is eighty degrees and summertime out there.

Hand-holding, the four of them were spread out as far as they could go without letting hands loose.

In the sweetest, highest voice, suddenly Aunt Babe went: "*Ring around the rosies . . .*" And her mom carried it on: "*Pocket full of posies . . .*"

"The two of you!" Aunt Digna exclaimed. "Sam, when will they grow up?"

Buhlaire saw Uncle Sam half-shrug. He was beaming at her mom. Buhlaire had never seen him look so bright and cheerful at anyone. *Like, if there was any place he'd most like to be, then right where he is, is it. Uncle Sam!*

Her mom was looking up at Uncle Sam with this wide-eyed, sweetest look of caring. With the warmest kind of feeling. It took Buhlaire's mind right out of her head. *Mom!* Then, a thought came. Then, Buhlaire knew something. *For sure.* She hadn't known before. Her insides did a flip-flop. All confused, she thought about her dad — *and Mom* . . . An idea hung there, caught on Uncle Sam — and her mom.

Bluezy was bareheaded, just the way Buhlaire liked to be with the cold. Uncle Sam, big as ever there was a man tall, had no hat, either. Both Digna and Babe had on blue wool caps — Babe had made them — pulled down over their ears. No style at all. Wearing them that way made the two of them look so comical. *I'm not laughing.*

Buhlaire suddenly felt real down inside herself. She came out from behind the tree all in a rush. Stumbling and half-sliding down the bank before she ever knew she would. The soft top-snow kept them from hearing her until she came bursting between Aunt Digna and Bluezy. She went into a falling skid and turned it at the last minute. So she'd hit Uncle Sam, hard, in his legs. She knew why she wanted to, she just didn't think about it. Had no idea she would do it until she was almost on him. Then, she felt glad. *Glad to hurt somebody — him.*

But Sam was quick. He leaped up off the ground

before she could hit him. She went sliding through his long legs. He grabbed her by the shoulders and pulled her back. Then, he lifted her off her feet, he was so strong. She hung there like a fish on one of his lines. And all of them were laughing at her.

"Oooh, Buhlaire," Aunt Digna said, "you scared me!" And kept laughing. "You looked so shocked when Sam lifted you up."

"That's who it was," said Aunt Babe. "Come so fast, I didn't know. How you doing, baby? What you doing running like that? Sam, if you got her up, put her down.

"We are out here, baby, because I wanted to smell the river," Aunt Babe continued. "I caught the scent of a tiny stream going by. I could smell its spring-green smell. No other like it! And water soon coming. Oh, lots-a water!"

Uncle Sam still had that pleased look on his face. It was warm and loving, a left-over look, not for her, Buhlaire thought. It faded as Buhlaire said, blisteringly, "Put me down. You big, overgrown — put me down!"

"Buhlaire," her mom said, warning her.

"You shut up," Buhlaire told her.

Sam dropped her as if she were a hot potato. And she cut out of the circle of them as fast as she could. She was on the outside by Digna and Babe.

"Buhlaire!" said surprised Aunt Babe. "That tone of voice — what is the matter with you?"

"Fresh, that's all," Digna said, hard and mean.

"Well, least I'm not some liar," Buhlaire said. She

wouldn't even bother mentioning how they were so prejudiced.

"That's enough, Buhlaire," her mom said.

"Why don't you be quiet?" she told her mom.

"I ought to slap you down," Digna said, "talking like that."

"Digna, will you be still?" her mom said.

"That's okay," Buhlaire said, "you're all the same. Just liars. And my name is Buhlly-Buhlly, like my dad calls me. Oh, by the way. My dad's not dead, like you always told me. See what he gave me?" She dug in the envelope and found the picture of her and her dad when she was small.

"He took the pictures and stuff because he wanted me with him. See? He wanted me to pay attention to him."

She smiled, head held high, and thrust the gift envelope for them to see.

They looked stunned. Aunt Digna looked away. Sam lowered his shoulders. He folded into himself like the wind had been knocked out of him. Her mom and Uncle Sam exchanged looks. Buhlaire watched and smirked into the air.

She sang, high as she could, in a pure, clear sound: "*I saw my daddy today. Down at the underpass. He gave me my back ti-i-me.*"

"Oh, Buhlaire," her mom said, in the saddest voice.

Buhlaire turned away from all of them. She headed for the house. In the fading, bluing winter light, home was becoming visible.

"You listen to me!" her mom said. "Buhlaire, you'd better hear me!"

Well! Snap! Diss you, too. Behind her, they all were coming up the riverbank.

"Digna, be careful, not so fast," said Aunt Babe.

"I got hold of you. Don't be so scared. Sam, take her other arm. You were doing fine," Digna told Babe. "Just don't get so frightened all of a sudden."

"I'm cold!" Aunt Babe whined. *Why won't they remember she is blind and it's scary?*

"Well, I know you're cold. Now hush. We'll be inside in a short minute," Digna said.

Buhlaire burst inside the house, leaving the door wide open. She put her gift envelope right in the middle of the table for all to see. She unslung her bookbag with the money deep inside and let it fall to the floor.

Oh, the house felt warm! She shivered, heat up her nose. *Haven't been home in forever, seems like*. Her hands just were numb, her wrists, frozen.

Bluezy came in with a rush of cold air. Aunt Digna with Aunt Babe was right on her heels. Digna shut the door.

"Where's Uncle Sam?" Buhlaire asked, smirking, looking at no one in particular. No one said anything. Her mom acted casual, as if to say, "Where Sam goes and what he does is up to Sam." *I couldn't care less. I can go off with my dad any time I want*.

"Buhlaire, sit down, let's talk," her mom said.

"I can stand up, thank you," she said, right back.

Her mom sighed. "All right, stand, then. But none of us meant to lie to you."

"Oh, right," Buhlaire said. "Saying my dad's dead when he's not — just a teeny, bitty, half-the-truth!" *When all this time* . . . If she said another word about it, she'd burst into tears.

Aunt Babe's hands came feeling along the chair back next to where Buhlaire was standing. She pulled out the chair and sat down; she still had her coat and hat on. Her hands reached for Buhlaire, caught her by the arms and pulled her down in the chair next to her. Just the touch of sweet Aunt Babe made Buhlaire have to sit. Made her murmur a shaky moan.

Babe folded Buhlaire to her. Buhlaire started crying, she couldn't help it. Then, her mom was touching, rubbing her shoulders. Buhlaire held on to Aunt Babe for dear life. *Never would hurt anybody. I know you wouldn't! Blind, but can see more better than most anybody.*

Aunt Babe's lips pressed into Buhlaire's Rasta curls. She began, "What it was, you were always still too young. It seemed like that. You're not but twelve now."

"Still too young," Aunt Digna added, "to be told about a father who wasn't right in his mind. That's why."

"Buhlaire, Junior had serious problems . . ." her mom said and faltered.

"Bublly-Bublly!" I hear you, Dad.

"I'm not saying it all was his fault," her mom

started again. "I mean, the troubles between us. But his mind went off on him. I was going to tell you all of it when you were old enough. Don't think I wasn't."

"You were going to bring him back to life?" came her voice. It sounded small and muffled against Aunt Babe.

"I was only trying to do what was right for you."

Right? Did you even want me? Not to tell the truth about my dad was right? "Junior Sims is my dad, isn't he?"

"Yes. I'm sorry, yes, he's your dad," Bluezy said.

Buhlaire lifted her head. Her face had streams of tears. She looked hard at her mom. "Because I don't care and I'm not sorry. I don't want any other dad. He's my dad!"

"People make mistakes . . ." Bluezy spoke carefully. "I made a couple of big mistakes. I was just eighteen and barely out of high school."

"You had me," Buhlaire sighed, "and you didn't want to stay married to my daddy." *Because of the vanilla?* She couldn't bring herself to say it. But it was there in the room. She blinked back tears. Aunt Babe held her tightly and stroked her hair.

"I knew he was a mistake, before we ever married. He and I were a mistake, before you were ever born," Bluezy said. "I was so young, and he was so handsome. . . ."

"Young girls make those kinds of serious errors," Aunt Digna said. "There's not a thing to be done about it."

No? "But to say he was dead!" Buhlaire cried. *How could you do that?*

"The way he was, it was hard to tell you, baby," Aunt Babe said. "Bluezy wanted to protect you from all that life he had."

"That's all we wanted. We didn't want you hurt," Aunt Digna said, almost in a whisper.

Amazed, Buhlaire shook her head. "You know what I think?" she asked. "I think you all were ashamed of me, too. Maybe Mom didn't want me." *Because I was so light, like him and his —*

"Buhlaire!" her mom said.

Well, she did know better than that. Buhlaire smiled a crooked smile, her eyes full of tears. "You wanted me, but all the time, you leave me," she said. "You would've told me about my dad, but you didn't, you lied. Would you have told me his mom or dad was vanilla?"

"Oh, Buhlaire!" her mom whispered. "I was afraid you'd want to know her. Sam, Buford, Sydney, Digna — they all had a different mother than your dad had. Junior's mom was their stepmother — nobody got along. She left. That's one reason Junior is the way he is. And also, I was afraid, the color, kids would tease you, use it against you."

"Well, at last," Aunt Babe said, and sighed a great breath of air.

"Better to have my dad dead and no back time, and that's not hurt?" Buhlaire asked. "I just wanted to know things. I didn't care what it was. I still don't. I just wanted to know!"

"I was going to tell you a lot of things when you turned sixteen," her mom said. "I will, too."

"I think you all are pretty weird," Buhlaire said seriously. "You're not at all like other people. You love me, you leave me. You cared for my dad, you divorced him." *You care for Sam.* She didn't say it. Not yet.

Digna spoke up. "Junior's a grown man," she said. "You should know he's done crazy stuff and some bad stuff, too — to get money for . . . for I don't know what all."

Buhlaire stared at Digna, thinking. But when she spoke, it was to her mom. "You ever been in the Shelter From *Any* Storm? Grady, my friend from school?" *Grady!* "His dad runs the shelter. And you know, all kinds of people stay in there. Even my dad. Grady told me he did."

"I see you've been spreading the word about this family all over town," Digna said.

Buhlaire ignored her. But she looked at them, shaking her head at them. *Grownups!* "At the shelter, nobody kills people off. They take care of them. And they don't care what color they are — chocolate, or vanilla, honey, mustard, caramel, you name it." Buhlaire sighed. "I'd rather have any kind of alive dad than any kind of dead one!"

"We thought we were doing right," said Aunt Babe.

"I'm not convinced we did so wrong," said Aunt Digna. "But this generation is not like ours. We didn't let children know everything, have nightmares. Maybe we played you cheap."

They fell silent, hearing the wind rise on the cold outside. Buhlaire looked out the windows and saw that the day had gone. Inside the house, the night came upon them, just as Aunt Digna turned on a light.

"Something's changed," said Aunt Babe.

"Night's come," Digna told her.

"Oh," Aunt Babe said. A shudder went through her; Buhlaire felt it.

Her mom said, "I think I learned from you today, Buhlaire."

Buhlaire answered, "He said he wanted you to stay home with him. How come you didn't? Was it because of Uncle Sam?"

The room seemed to get so still, the quiet felt as if it would hurt her ears. She unwound herself from warm and soft Aunt Babe. That broke the stunned silence into pieces. She sat up straight, and looked at her mom.

After a moment, Bluezy had something to say: "It would have hurt him too much. I couldn't do that."

"What's that supposed to mean?" Buhlaire asked.

"Can't make up one's mind, I do believe," Aunt Babe said, in a faraway voice.

Her mom never answered Babe. She said, "Sam and I are close friends. But I won't marry."

"You are extreme-weird," Buhlaire said. "You should be with who you love. I'm twelve, and even I know that."

"Twelve going on twenty," Aunt Digna said.

"I guess," her mom said, answering Buhlaire.

"But I worry about this child not having a father," Digna said.

"I have a father," Buhlaire shot right back.

"I mean, a real father," Digna said, and was at once sorry.

In an instant, Buhlaire was on her feet. She grabbed her envelope off the table and got the straps of her bookbag in her hand. "I'm like you all," she said, straightening up. "I do what I want. My dad needs me to help him, and I'm going to help him. Don't try to stop me."

12

Gifts

She stared at it. All the stuff from her dad she had laid out on her desk. *Back time has come home.*

Just looking at the pictures and feeling the medals, slowly, she remembered things. Medals never meant as much as the music. Music came to her, and being all dressed up, with her mom, Aunt Babe, and Aunt Digna. An awards program in school. People clapping. She almost pictured that. Was sure she remembered that. It wasn't the medals, but what they stood for. It was being with people who admired her that meant something to Buhlaire. It was being recognized and paid attention to.

She couldn't get enough of how she and her dad looked when she was this real little kid. *Little outside child.* Her dad had been a very good-looking, special-looking man, she thought. *Hair all cut. Poor him. Clean and neat, back then. Maybe he can look that way again. But, word. Back time won't come back for real, not for me. I can't be way little again. But he might get better. Crazy people don't stay crazy all the time — I don't think so.*

* * *

That evening, they came to her bearing gifts. They brought her their reasons and good sense. She knew that's how they thought. She sat moving around the pictures, admiring her mom, who seemed always young. Not picking up the pictures, but positioning them over and over. Aunt Babe came in twice.

Buhlaire never heard Aunt Babe coming. She saw her hands first on the door frame. Fingers like some pale vines climbing and spreading.

Aunt Babe came in and sat down on the bed. "Buhlaire, come sit by me."

She didn't want to, but she couldn't say no to Aunt Babe. "What is it?" Buhlaire asked.

"But let me tell you," Babe said. "It will be a hard, wet spring. Don't go, baby."

Buhlaire held her breath, not to give it away. Finally, she said, "Aunt Babe, how come you think that?"

Babe got up and without another word, she went out. She left fifty dollars on the bedspread. Two twenties and a ten. Buhlaire wouldn't touch it. She hadn't asked for the money. It was as if Aunt Babe could figure her out any time she wanted to.

Babe came back about a half hour later. "Know I love you, baby," she said. "I'm going to bed." She dropped two twenties in the doorway. Buhlaire stared at them. It was longer than a few minutes before she picked them up. She put them with the fifty dollars and folded them all in a small wad. She put the wad with the other money in the envelope from the bank, inside her bookbag.

Bluezy came in around ten o'clock. Buhlaire was curled up in her bed under the covers. She hadn't changed her clothes.

"If you take off that jumpsuit, I'll wash it with my things," her mom said.

Buhlaire stared at her. "You are going to wash my jumpsuit by yourself? Aunt Digna break an arm?"

"Very funny."

"Are you going to be here when I wake up in the morning?"

Her mom gave her a look. "I heard about you and Digna fighting."

You didn't answer the question. Buhlaire looked away.

"My fault for leaving you like that," Bluezy said.

"You always leave me like that," Buhlaire said, right back. *No, not always.*

Her mom looked concerned. "I can see you're upset about it. Are you feeling sad and depressed?" Bluezy asked.

Something about the way she said it made Buhlaire giggle. "Sad and depressed? Take a Doozie-Dozie!" she said.

"Huh, right," said her mom. "Take a pi-ill. Well, good, let's laugh at us before someone else does. But do you think you can't take it?" Bluezy asked. "Because, if you feel like, over the edge, I'll come home for a while."

"Oh, I'm not going to flip out and take drugs or something."

"Well, good," her mom said.

"You are *weird*!"

"Puh-leaze, stop with the 'weird,'" her mom said.

"Well, you are."

"Listen. I think you're a gorgeous kid. And I'm glad you care so much about your dad. I truly am. But you have to know something, Buhlaire, even if it hurts. Junior is rot and pain."

"Thanks a lot, Mom," Buhlaire said. She could have said more. She felt like hurting her mom for it. Cursing at her, the way she had at Aunt Digna. But she held it back. *I'm not some kid*. "He's my dad," she whispered. She hurt, more than she could ever say.

"No more not telling the truth to you," her mom said. "Whatever you are thinking to do, think about it knowing who and what he is."

"I won't lie to you, either," Buhlaire said. "I'm going to help him."

"I'd appreciate it if you'd stay away from him. Stay away from out there. If I have to, I'll have Sam keep you here."

She looked at her mom. Saw she meant it.

"I don't like you much," Buhlaire told her.

"I'm sure that's true, for the moment. Nevertheless."

"Nevertheless," Buhlaire said, "I will leave here for good, if you sic Uncle Sam on me. Grady, my friend, goes out there with me. We got caught in a whiteout. And my dad saved us."

"Really?" her mom said.

"He sure did," Buhlaire told her. "He knew where I was, and he got us in the underpass and built a fire. And he even gave us soup, both of us. My dad was real nice to us."

"So," her mom said. "Maybe he's getting better."

"Word," Buhlaire said. "He's my *dad*. And he's not mental all the time. So Uncle Sam better stay away from both of us."

Her mom sighed, leaned her head against the wall. She was tall and pretty in beige slacks and a dark gray sweater. Looking like somebody's daytime jeep-wagon mom, thought Buhlaire. Bluezy in disguise!

"You should know that Sam, all of us, have helped him over the years," her mom said. "Sam pays for his hospital and everything, even when they throw him in jail, each time. But Junior refuses to come in 'off the road' as he calls it. He's not able to stay inside of any place for long. He gets sane real fast when they confine him, though. That's just the way he is. And out there, he's prone to hurt himself."

"That's his mental illness," Buhlaire said.

"I think probably so. But it's hard to know which came first, the egg or the chicken," Bluezy said.

"I like him," Buhlaire said. *I love my dad!* "I think he likes me a lot, too."

"Oh, he loved the idea of you," her mom said. "He always said you were the most beautiful child.

And, Buhlaire, he always returns to Plain City. He never goes out of the state."

After her mother went out, and Buhlaire was still thinking about her dad, Aunt Digna came in. She didn't say much. There was this tension Buhlaire felt between them. Aunt Digna checked the window, looked around the room. Buhlaire could tell Digna couldn't bring herself to say any sorrys. Neither could Buhlaire. *Maybe that's the way it has to be with us.*

Digna said, "Good-night, baby," and left. *I'm not a baby. Tell you one time, too. Quit calling me that.*

All night, Buhlaire worried. She'd wake up deep under the covers, thinking about her dad. She could practically feel the cold out there, the way it must be. The terrible dark at night out there that must almost come alive in the deep, ice-cold underpass, where the blue light of winter night and snow could never penetrate. *But they have fires.* She consoled herself with that. *I am like my dad, can't stand the indoors for long. Have to stride the land. Just an outside child!*

She went to sleep with fear and emptiness in the pit of her stomach. She woke up, afraid for her dad all over again. She went back to sleep and woke up again, terrified, this time. Whether dreaming, she didn't know.

But she woke up with her eyes already wide open. She knew there was somebody in the room. This little girl all dressed up, going around and around with her arms straight out from her shoulders. Buhlaire felt sick with dizziness.

Sick with dread. And then, slowly, she came back to herself. She hadn't really been awake. It was a nightmare she'd had. It made her feel awful.

She closed her eyes, to face what was real. Angry at her mom, but she knew it wasn't her mom's fault, none of it. It wasn't her dad's, or that little girl's. Me, she thought, the little girl. You can't blame anybody.

It's the hand you're dealt, Aunt Digna'd say. I say you can't change back time. Back time stays back, that's all.

Mom loves me. It was like the little child in her was telling her true. *My dad loves me, as much as he can. My poor daddy. Anyway, both of them are mine.*

In the morning, she woke up tired, still worried about him.

She spent a half hour putting warm clothes in her bookbag and trying to squeeze her books in on top of them. *It's not going to work.*

She set aside a warm sweater and a pair of wool knee socks to put on under the jumpsuit. She knew she would be too warm all morning in school. *Have to go in first thing. Have to take a signed excuse for yesterday to the office. But I'll leave by lunchtime. Grady! Been so long since I saw you last. Don't know what will happen out there. I don't want to go away. I want to be with my dad, but I don't want to leave here. Oh, well. I'll face it when I face it.*

Her mom brought her the jumpsuit, knocking first, before she came in.

"You're still here!" Buhlaire said, faking surprise.

"Good morning, pretty bird. Better wash up," her mom sang.

"Don't tell me what to do-oo," Buhlaire sang back. She went swiftly out the door. Took a quick shower. The house was coolish.

"Mom!" she called from the shower. "Write me an excuse, please. I cut school to see my dad yesterday."

"Hurry up," Bluezy called. "I have to go soon."

Where are you going? Cleveland. I don't care. I mean, it doesn't matter where. It was as if she couldn't stay mad at her mom. She was truly glad of that.

Her mom had to leave after having breakfast with her. "Be back in three days." She handed Buhlaire the written, signed excuse. "Don't make cutting a habit."

"Thank you," Buhlaire said, taking it.

"Going down to Memphis and end up over at Louisville," her mom said. "You got what for?"

"I'm giving some money to my dad," Buhlaire said easily. It rolled off her tongue. "I have some money left in the bank."

Her mom frowned and said, "You give it of your own generous heart. I understand that, I do. You don't expect any payback. But please, don't give him too much."

"I won't," Buhlaire said, surprised her mom went along with the idea.

They stood close in the hall. Buhlaire moved, leaned her head onto Bluezy's chest. Bluezy's arms came quickly to encircle her. And slowly, Buhlaire let go of the resentment at her mom's leaving. "You smell nice," Buhlaire told her mom, her arms clasped behind Bluezy's neck. She rested her head on Bluezy's chest.

"Yum, yum, yum," said her mom, kissing her cheek.

"By-yie," Buhlaire murmured. *Hate to see you go. Uncle Sam's taking you?* She realized she knew so little about her mom's work. "Does Uncle Sam drive you?"

"Just over to the airport, then I take a little plane."

"No kidding?"

Her mom laughed. "I love you," she whispered in her ear. "Buhlaire, ask Sam to take you out there."

"No," Buhlaire said. "Just me and Grady go out there. Mom, does Uncle Sam like me?"

"Of course he does."

"I didn't know," she said. "I can never tell, his face is always . . ."

"What?"

"Like . . . flat and still. Like a frozen . . . river." *But a river runs . . .*

Her mom sighed. "I . . . I do care about Sam. And I'd never leave you for even a day if I didn't know he was here keeping an eye out."

"I didn't know he did that. He doesn't follow me out there, does he?"

"No, I wouldn't think so. But he knows what goes

on. He always has you in mind. Buhlaire, you've been a great kid, maybe a little too by yourself, but still a great kid."

"Well, I'm not a kid anymore."

"Yes, you are still a kid, my baby girl."

"Word, straight up. Buhlaire-Marie is growing older."

"Really? I think I'd better meet this . . . Grady person," her mom said.

"Mo-om!" Buhlaire screamed. "I didn't mean like that!"

"Ouch, my ears! Okay, but I want to meet him anyway sometime," Bluezy said.

"Next time," Buhlaire said. "Can he come over, I mean, anytime?"

"I guess so, why not?"

"Tell Aunt Digna, or she won't like it."

"I'll tell Sam, let him take care of Digna." They smirked at each other.

"Oooh!" Buhlaire hollered.

Bluezy hushed her. "You want Digna to yell at us?"

Buhlaire laughed into her hands. Then, her mom was gone. And she was left to grab her stuff and get to school.

Lunchtime, she sauntered out, like she was going to have lunch in town. Grady followed her. When they were on the far side, he caught up with her. Now she didn't mind if he walked with her. No one she knew would see them over here. Just her dad.

They could hear the interstate, then farther along

she saw her dad walking the landscape ahead. Knew it was him. He strutted like a soldier on parade. *My dad.*

She liked to stride. So did Grady. They were soon closer; she saw her dad had on this long greatcoat. He was wearing a cap, just like the kind Northern soldiers wore in the Civil War. She recognized it from pictures in the American history unit at school.

"Where'd he get that getup?" Grady said, laughing.

"Don't you laugh at him!" she said through her teeth. And Grady shut up.

Her dad had on high leather boots, like horseback riding boots, she thought. He looked better now than he had when she first saw him. But like from — *some back time. Man!* His Rasta twists pushed the hat up high. It did not sit well atop that gray, cornstalk-color hair, long and thick, twisting like snakes around his neck. Nothing about him fit together.

He saw them coming. If he'd been on a horse, he would have whipped that horse and galloped to them. As it was, he took great leaping steps, swinging his arms. He swooped down and caught Buhlaire in a big bearhug.

"Buhlly-Buhlly, how you doin'? You are looking good — looking so good. I'm so glad, so glad to see you. You know, heh, heh. You know?"

"Hi, Daddy. Yeah, I know. I'm glad to see you, too. You remember Grady."

He looked at Grady as though Grady were a Confederate spy. He looked mean at Grady. "You get out the way, over there!" Her dad pointed away from them. Grady moved some few feet over to Buhlaire's right.

"Daddy, that's not nice," she said. "He's my friend."

"Don't get me mad. Get me mad!"

"Okay, calm down," she said softly. "I brought you something." *Acting like he's crazy!* She felt afraid, watchful of him. Yet she didn't think he'd hurt her.

Now he grinned, smiling like an angel from ear to ear. "Ooooh," he said. "You brought me my stash, I bet. Did you? Did you?"

"I sure did. But let's not let anybody see." She took her bookbag off and dug deep for the bank envelope full of money.

"Daddy. This is a lot of money." She looked around. Grady wasn't staring at them, but he had to hear what they were saying.

"I know you did me up good, Buhlly-Buhlly. I know-I know," her dad said.

"There's almost three hundred dollars," Buhlaire told him. *Part of it Aunt Babe gave. Daddy, don't lose it. I worked so hard for it — mowed lawns — Dad, don't throw it away, please.* "Do you have some place to put it?" She kept her hand with the envelope inside her bag.

"Under my clothes," he said. "Got a waistband to keep my money in."

"Good," she said, relieved. He wasn't so crazy. "I'll slide it inside your coat."

They stood close together. She slid the envelope out and to him.

He had it inside his clothing while they laughed and pretended to talk. It was done that quickly. "Let's cut on out," he said. "And you can't come!" he yelled at Grady so suddenly, Grady was startled and on his guard. Her dad turned back to her, said, "That much money we can find us a good hiding place."

Oh, Daddy. No place to hide, Dad. All this time, last night, too, she'd been trying to figure it out. Make up her mind. "Daddy," she said. She shook her head. "I never thought you really would want me to go with you." *Don't want to let my money go — can't go with it — can I?* "I mean, I thought about it. I thought I would go. But then, I wasn't sure . . ." *Don't lie.* She knew she wasn't big enough. "I . . . can't go with you, Daddy." But part of her wanted to.

He looked at her, peered at her so hard, she had to turn away a moment. "Aunt Babe needs me," she pleaded. "Nobody understands her like I do." *That's just an excuse. Oh, man.*

"Ohhhh," he said. "Babe. I remember Babe. How's Babe! How's she doin'?"

"She's almost blind!" Buhlaire cried, feeling sick inside, using her Aunt Babe like that. "She can't see hardly anything." *Dad, I hate to let you down!* "I have to stay." *What else can I do?*

She tried to be kind. "Daddy." She liked calling him that. "I . . . don't think I could make it 'on the road' like you do. It takes lots of courage. I'd be afraid." *There. I said it. It's true. I'd be too scared. And scared to be all dirty and hungry.*

He stood there, looking off into the day. Looking somehow proud. He had his hands on his hips, staring at another gray sky. He looked odd — as if none of his parts, his head of hair, his hat and boots, coat, longish body — none of them came together smoothly. But at last he nodded and turned to her.

"Buhlly-Buhlly. Gotcha!" he murmured, so sweet-looking with his loving eyes on her.

Daddy. She hugged him around the waist, closed her eyes against him. She made herself stand his sour smell. *My dad. You can't help it*. He let his arms wrap around her. "I understand," he said, in his man's sane voice. "It's okay. And you need to go to school. I'll be all right."

"Daddy, I'll come and see you — how will I find you?"

He grinned. "I'll be back," he said.

"And when you need anything," she said, "well, I'll come."

He held her at arm's length and gazed at her. "You are so pretty. Pretty. Beautiful." His voice caught. His eyes filled so quickly. He turned his head away to shake it off. *Dad, don't cry*. He gave her shoulders a squeeze. "Got to get my stuff," he said. He flicked his hand back at her, waving behind his back at her as he walked off.

"Bye, Daddy."

So. Gone with my money. I worked so hard. So, maybe

he is a con. But he's still my dad — face it! She cried inside.

Her dad walked on, very proud-looking in his getup, out of sight in the underpass. She didn't want to see him come out. She hurried, rushing on her way to school, striding. They had to make time, she and Grady.

"I'm glad that's over," Grady said. "You okay?"

She nodded. But it would never be over with her and her dad. It would never be anywhere near okay inside her. *If I can see him and be sure he's all right . . . I can live with it.* All of a sudden, she felt old. An old teen.

"He didn't even thank you for the money," Grady said.

"Not your business, bwoy," she told him. *He doesn't have to thank me. He's my dad.* She didn't say much the rest of the way.

13

Late January Thaw

She was dreaming she was a gray flapping cloth girl. And she was talking in the dreaming. *Makes sense we live in the Water Houses.*

Been raining forever. I'll write that down for Mom to sing. The rain was with her. She heard something, sounding bulging and full out of its mouth.

"Huh? Mom?" Buhlaire came fully awake, calling her mom. She forgot the dream at once. She knew what day it was. Saturday. Always raining. It was more than a week and a half, she figured, since she'd seen her dad. Soon after, the rain had started. It poured. It seeped and creeped into everything. For days, it drenched, melted everything. Hardly a bit of snow was left. Just dirty gray patches and slippery slicks of it along the swollen river.

Buhlaire tried hard, and she remembered the dream. The cloth girl hadn't been pinned to the clothesline. *Me.* She had been holding on with her hands. *It was me, holding on. I wasn't ever going to fall. Felt like a wet sheet flapping. Only, I was me, a gray girl. Funny!* The dream had been dark with rain. She kept thinking she'd never get dry.

Rain was coming down for real. Must've rained all night, she thought. Such misty rain, slapping at everything. It fouled the air. *Smells like wet-dog-fur putrid, soaking wet piles of funky garbage.* Rain made her angry. She wanted sun and light.

"Mom?" She's not even here. *Shoot! Think of it — writing a song in your sleep! "Been raining forever," she sang in her head, "Turn it down, turn it down . . ."*

We could've written the song together, shoot. Anger, smoldering.

A bulging, croaking sound came from outside. *I heard that in my sleep!* It kept on. "Bulge-bulge. Blope," Buhlaire muttered, matching the sound.

She pulled on stretch pants and a sweater over her night shirt. *What day is it — yeah! Saturday!* She had her socks on already; she had slept in them. And went to the living room. The door to Aunt Babe's room was open, as was the front door. A screen door let in fresh air that was not quite cold. She shivered, for it was cool enough. *January thaw doesn't mean heat yet. Just, not freezing, I guess — when did Uncle Sam take the storm door out? I never see what's going on. Man! It's not even February and it's raining.*

Glumly she sniffed and could smell the outside. *Must be fifty-five degrees. Musty and pukey. Yuk!*

She opened the screen and stepped out on the porch stoop. Saw the drenching, foggy rain. Heard noises, rising around her.

Things. Buhlaire screamed. She couldn't move.

They were all over the place. They jumped up at her. They leaped at her. Some went "Blope!" and plopped down. Frogs. There looked to be thousands, multiplied and magnified in Buhlaire's shocked imagination.

Sitting in the midst of all that green and slippery wet was little Dale, the three-year-old Aunt Sydney Sims took care of. He had on striped flannel pajamas with feet in them. He was all scrunched up on the top step of the porch. Just kind of sobbing, sweeping his hands back and forth over the backs of the little things. He barely touched their backs. But every time he swept them, they went flying every which way.

Buhlaire screamed, "Ohhh, uuugh!" trying to stand on one foot. "Don't touch me, oooh!"

The little kid reached for her, wailing. She couldn't bring herself to step on the things to get to him. Frogs. Hundreds of the slick and slimy uglies, jumping and practically flying, and landing every which way.

Buhlaire covered her eyes, peeked through her fingers, and kicked with her feet. Things, and they crawled over her toes. She screamed, "Aunt Digna! Oh! Oh! Help!"

Now Dale was frantic, bouncing up and down on his little behind. Holding his arms up high above the frogs. One leaped right under him when he bounced up.

"E-ooh! Oh, shoot, no!" Buhlaire imagined a splat when the kid bounced down.

Digna came out the door, stepping carefully. "Yelling like that? What's wrong with you — you'll wake the dead." She saw Buhlaire had one foot on top of the other, hands over her eyes. "You better watch what you're doing. And get over it. Just nothing but frogs, goodness."

And water. Buhlaire peeked out. She'd been too busy being terror-stricken to see it. She could hardly make sense of it.

"Diggie, Diggie," cried the little kid, looking miserably at Digna and stretching his arms out to her.

"Didn't I tell you to stay inside with Babe?" Aunt Digna said to him. "You had to come out here and scare yourself to death. I can't turn my back for a minute with you. Be glad when Sydney gets back from town." She added, "I told Aunt Babe to watch him. I forgot, she can't see nothing. Come on, I said!" she told the kid. "I got some oatmeal. Now be careful, Dale, watch where you're stepping." Digna smiled at Buhlaire. "He's cute as a button!"

The kid threaded his way through the frogs jumping around him. He didn't take his eyes off his feet. He kept his arms out to Digna. "Now, I can't hold you," she said. "You've gotten too big for Digna to carry. Come on. Watch out! Don't let the froggies in!"

"Foggies in," Dale murmured, hypnotized by their croaking and jumping.

The whole world. Changes. Even with all the croaking noise, Buhlaire was also hypnotized, but by what lay before her.

"Well, it happened before, when you were way little," Digna said, standing inside the screen door.

She followed Buhlaire's gaze. "Babe said it would come one day again — January thaw. She loves predicting. I suppose if each year you say it will flood, and one year it does, why then you get the crown."

"I can't believe it," Buhlaire said breathlessly. She glanced around at Digna. Digna's hands combed through little Dale's black hair. He stood in front of her at the screen, calmly looking out.

Buhlaire turned back to the scene in front of the house. Vaguely, she was aware that Aunt Digna and her charge had gone off to the kitchen. But she was amazed by what was spread out before her like something she couldn't have dreamed. *The whole world is water.* That's what it looked like. The land, the hard ground was flooded everywhere. True, in this last part of January, the weather had warmed above freezing. Rain kept on. Ice and snow melted. The river rose. But things changed over that length of time, so she hadn't really noticed. But she did know the ground down here got really squishy off the walkways. Deep down it might stay frozen while the river thawed. And there might come a cold snap again before spring.

Now there was no Montgomery Falls River as such. It had spread far and wide. There was no land. The sycamores had no ground. Everything was flooded and flowing. The trees floated in a chocolate water flood. The houses had waterways under them.

Tops of high bushes could be seen, but that's all. Frogs climbed out of the water onto the steps, and up trees. She thought she saw a snake hanging down from a branch, off a ways. The Water Houses on their high stilts seemed to be just inches above the water. *My lord!* All of it hit her, that this was truly flood time. *It is extreme-serious.*

She just stood in the frogs, getting used to them now, and stared. It took some adjusting to. *Took the ground right from under us.* When she looked at the moving water, she got dizzy. So she concentrated on the trees. They were what made it all so strange, sticking out of the water. And boats!

There were motorboats; she heard their motors before she saw them. Off in the distance, a boat with two paddlers was brimming with folks. One held a yipping dog. Somebody was hollering, "Help, we're going to fill up!" Somebody else said, "Hush! Set still 'fore you drown us all!" A helicopter went over, just above the tree line. Buhlaire climbed over the many frogs, and got in the house without hurting them. "I swear, I can't live with those creatures!"

"Buhlaire." It was Aunt Babe.

"Aunt Babe! Aunt Babe!" Buhlaire was so excited, she could hardly stand. She sat down beside Aunt Babe on the couch. "It is unbelievable. You should see it."

"I can feel it," Babe said, grinning. "I told everybody it would come. Flood time. Nothing like it. Feel it coming in the first whiff of warm air. I knew it would be the thaw time, too, because I felt it even in my sleep. Tell me how it looks out there, baby."

Buhlaire told her. "Aunt Babe, it is like nothing

in the world." She leaned real close for comfort, and Babe put her arm around her. "With trees," Buhlaire went on, "just wading in the water. Houses, holding their skirts barely high from the wet. And frogs! Millions and millions of frogs."

Babe laughed. "Sure sounds like it. All night, too, they have to balump-balump, back and forth to each other. They are something. I suspect they come right out from under briers and rocks and things. Everything, every hibernating critter out of the ground. And rabbits, and moles. And people off the ground, too. Flood time makes you see how small we are and how big the world is that can change and come down on you in a minute. Everything, flooded."

Suddenly, Buhlaire had a thought that made her cover her mouth and cry. *My dad! My poor dad! Maybe he's not out there. But what if he is? He'll drown!* "Aunt Babe, I don't know what's happened to my dad."

"Don't you worry about a thing, baby. They are out there," Aunt Babe comforted her. "Uncle Sam's got his boat out, with Uncle Buford. They've taken Sydney and some people over there into town for food. Dale's mom is coming back later. I thought I was watching him until Sydney got back. Hee, hee! He was marching the chair around. Then he must've run out. I watched that chair for half an hour! Thought it was him. I did wonder why he was standing so still, though, goodness. I don't know where I put my glasses last night."

"Aunt Babe, they're on top of your head."

"Oh!" Babe said, laughing. "Do you suppose I slept with them like that?" She sighed and put them on.

Buhlaire sat there, getting sick with worry for her dad, when she heard a boat come near. She got up and tore to her room to get her shoes and boots on. She grabbed a scarf, her gloves, and a jacket. *Maybe it's Uncle Sam! He's got to help me hunt for my dad.* She got everything on in fast time.

The boat was across the way from her by the time she got back outside. It was in the wading trees. It was going slowly. *All this! Water and boats. Never seen anything like it.* She watched it go over there to the other side where one far bank should have been.

The boat went slowly for a while, then the motor seemed to drone, and it came across toward her.

It was Uncle Sam and Uncle Buford with Aunt Sydney and some people. The boat was full of stuff. It came nearer. Buhlaire wanted to yell, "Uncle Sam!" but thought better of it. The boat kept coming. It stopped at one of the other Water Houses first. Uncle Buford got out and took some things, supplies, with him. There was another boat over there. He put the supplies in the other boat, got in, and took off.

Now Aunt Digna was out looking, too, with the little child, Dale, by the hand. The frogs were all around, jumping and croaking. Buhlaire paid them no mind. She watched the boat. She saw it was her dad in there. *Oh, I'm so glad!*

"Don't say anything loud that might upset him," Aunt Digna said.

"I won't. I won't," Buhlaire said.

"He's all right," Aunt Digna told her. "Sam went looking for him first thing."

Sam brought the boat around to them. Aunt Digna took a line from him and tied it to the stoop post.

"Daddy," Buhlaire said.

"Syd-ee," Dale called. It was Aunt Sydney in the boat.

Junior Sims looked exhausted. He smiled weakly at Buhlaire.

"Please, can he come in?" Buhlaire asked Aunt Digna.

"He won't come in," she said in Buhlaire's ear. "I'm surprised he got in the boat with Sam."

Then, Junior Sims reached for Buhlaire.

Uncle Sam said to her, "He wouldn't go to the shelter until he found out you were all right."

"I'm all right, Daddy," she said.

"Buhlly-Buhlly," he said, taking her arm. There was nothing for her to do but get in the boat with him. Then she helped Sydney out and onto the porch. Aunt Digna handed little Dale to Sydney.

"Did you bring me my stuff?" Aunt Digna asked Sam.

"I bought all you said," Sam told her.

Digna made three trips inside with it.

"Distribute from here. Buford will help you and Sydney," Uncle Sam told her.

"We'll make chili in case people run short and can't get out," Digna said.

They went on, then, she and her dad and Uncle Sam. Her dad sat in the middle beside her. Uncle Sam sat in the back, running the motor and guiding the boat. Being on so much water was real scary. She took her dad's hand. His hand was cold, and he was acting strange. He was watching Uncle Sam as best he could out of the corner of his eye. *My dad doesn't like Uncle Sam.*

"Were you flooded out?" she asked her dad. He was too watchful to say anything. It hurt her when he acted crazy like that.

Uncle Sam said, "A bunch of them were on top of the underpass, outside, soaking wet."

Buhlaire let go of her dad to hold on as another boat passed, causing waves. Branches, clothing, floated in the water. *Wow! Careful!* Uncle Sam slowed and stopped in the shallow water to pick up stranded people all along the way. The boat was soon full. Everybody talked at once, telling about their narrow escapes out of the water.

"This one guy got bit by a moccasin. Helicopter took him out."

"While ago, I had frogs in my boots. I heard they once called this Frogtown, and now I know why," another said.

Her dad sat, huddled against her. She saw that behind her, Uncle Sam had his eye on them. "We're going to take everybody to the shelter," he said, generally. "Get something hot in you there."

It wasn't long before they all had to get out and walk up to Midway. Uncle Sam held the boat still. He gave everybody a hand out, except her dad. Her dad wouldn't let Sam touch him. *And they're almost brothers. Half-brothers!*

Once there, she and her dad went into the shelter together. Inside, kids were crying, tired out and scared. Just noise echoing. All was confusion, with people milling everywhere. Uncle Sam went off to find Mr. Terrell. Buhlaire looked for Grady. Anxiously, she searched all around. She couldn't find him. Her dad found him.

"That's your boy, that boy with you," he said. Grady came and got them at the same time Uncle Sam came back. "I knew you'd come," Grady said, whispering. "There's a place off my dad's office. He wants your dad to take it."

"Oh, thank you," Buhlaire told him. "That's great."

"Thanks," said Uncle Sam.

Her dad jerked his head around, saw Sam, and closed in on himself.

"We can give everybody at least a dry shirt and pants." It was Mr. Terrell telling the people that. He came over to them. Nodded at Buhlaire and Sam.

"Lots of wet, sick people," he said. He looked exhausted. "Take him back over there," he said to Sam. But Junior wouldn't move. He was still watching Sam out of the corner of his eye.

"We'd better go," Sam said to Buhlaire. When she was about to protest, she saw caution in his eyes. He shook his head, warning her. Then, she knew. Her dad would do nothing as long as Uncle Sam was there.

She took her dad's arm. "I have to go back to Aunt Babe," she told him.

He seemed to relax, then, smiled wanly down at the floor. "Daddy, I'll be back as soon as I can. But you need to get out of those wet clothes right now."

"I know-I know," he murmured. Then, he looked at her in a cool, solid gaze. "You be all right?" he asked.

"Daddy, I'm fine!" She smiled at him, made him understand. *He worries for me*. Suddenly, she realized he'd gotten a haircut. Even though his clothes were drying on him, they seemed to be better clothes, and not so raggedy. It looked as if he'd spent some of the money she'd given him — in the right way. "Daddy. See you later!"

He held her gaze and smiled at her. "So long," he said. He gave her his wave behind his back and went off with Mr. Terrell.

"I have to work," Grady apologized, having to leave them.

"We're going on," Uncle Sam said.

"See you! I'll be back tomorrow to see my dad," she told Grady, waving. *My friend.*

They returned to the boat. She sat in the middle by herself. She had her hands up her sleeves all the way. It was funny. Everything was like it was over. Everything had changed, too. But not for the bad. *It's exciting, life is.*

Water spread out in every direction. It had climbed the lower part of Midway, but it didn't come near any stores. There was brown water flowing very far, coming off surrounding fields and everywhere. *Summer's coming. Yeah, word! Sure is a big world. We're just part of it. Me and my dad. Lots of people have . . . troubles. Not everybody is lucky as me. I found my dead dad alive. Ha!*

Uncle Sam. I guess he's pretty okay. He's different, like the rest of us.

Mom is . . . busy being Mom! Oh, I don't blame her. But I want her with me, too. How can she be both places? Maybe when I'm sixteen — will we sing together? Oh, I hope. I'll study real hard. Maybe we'll become Bluezy and Little Blue! Ha! Wonder if she'll dance the fans for me, ever. Wonder if she and Uncle Sam will just not sneak around, but out in the open, be in love. Oh, romantic! Wonder if ever she and my dad. No, he's the way he is. Does he stay that way, or get better? I think he stays that way.

It was a bitter pill for her to think so. *He's been that way so long. And always needs help. I don't think*

I'll give him any more money. Oh, but I hope he used some of it to get himself a nice room. I'll ask Uncle Sam what to do. Mom says Uncle Sam watches out for me. So maybe one day I can tell him things. Tell him I want to see more of my mom. Maybe sometime he'll take me to see her on the road. Things can change!

I love my Aunt Babe, true, true! I don't want her to be afraid of the grayness. I'll push it back for her, me, being with her. And I don't really mind Aunt Digna. She can be a real pill, though. I guess we'll always fight. You have to watch her. But she takes care of things.

You sit in the boat, and it goes, and the motor goes. You forget it can't go by itself. It just looks like it does. There has to be somebody there to drive it. Uncle Sam!

She turned around and gave him a grin. All this time, he had his eye on her. The boat slowed, headed over toward shallow water.

"You want to help me pick up some more people? It might take up most the day. They always want you to help them do something," Uncle Sam said.

"Sure, okay!" she said, pleased he wanted her around.

She got her balance and stood up to help a woman holding a brown puppy. The woman's feet were in the water. She had to wade the water to them. "Lordy, Lordy, Lordy," she said over and over again.

"You're all right now," Buhlaire told her. "We've gotcha!"

It went like that the whole day. They were so busy. *Good, great day! Helping just all kinds of folks.*

She thought about Grady and how he helped folks there at the shelter. *Guess I'll be seeing a lot of him. It's not so hard to make a friend. I can do it again, I bet I can.*

Now she was used to the boat rocking, and strangers, sitting so close to her. Soon it seemed like the most normal thing to be moving along where dripping trees stood, reflected in high flooding.

Finally, she and Uncle Sam were by themselves in the boat and finished for the day. She was so tired! But her mind kept going on about things as she stared over the side.

Water running. You can't stop it. You can't stop rain, or fishes, running. Well. It was like I was asleep. Just hibernated, way down deep under.

Still water runs deep. You can't stop running water. Brown, running water. It will seep away. I'll be out of the flood time, on dry land. Little frog, me. Hop. Blope.

You can't stop, me.

The flood's washed all the dirt away, she thought. Everything's come clean!

Suddenly her stomach made a real loud roar. *E-ooh! Embarrassing!*

"*I heard that!*" Uncle Sam grinned all over his face.

"I forgot to eat!" she told him. At once, she had a terrific hunger. And then she laughed. Her high soprano pealed over the brown, shimmery, wastewater, breaking among flooded sycamores. The shrill sound of it emptied out into nature. Softly, slowly, it faded. She was left feeling thoughtful, and as calm as the day's quiet going.

Uncle Sam let her steer the boat home. It was suppertime.

About the Author

VIRGINIA HAMILTON grew up in Yellow Springs, Ohio, the town to which her grandfather came when he left Virginia as an escaped slave. She published more than thirty books for young readers, including *M.C. Higgins, the Great; Sweet Whispers, Brother Rush;* and *Bluish.* Among her many honors, she was awarded the Newbery Medal, three Newbery Honors, the National Book Award, the Hans Christian Andersen Medal, the Coretta Scott King Award, the Edgar Allan Poe Award, the Regina Medal, the Boston Globe–Horn Book Award, the Laura Ingalls Wilder Medal, a MacArthur Fellowship, and three honorary doctorates.

Acknowledgments

Permission was granted to print passages from the following songs: "Bridge Over Troubled Water," by Paul Simon, copyright © 1969 by Paul Simon and reprinted by permission of Paul Simon Music; "It Ain't Fair," by Ronnie Miller, copyright © 1968 by Cotillion Music Inc. All rights are administered by Warner-Tamerlane Publishing Corp., all rights reserved; and "Let It Be," by John Lennon and Paul McCartney, copyright © MacLen Music. All rights controlled and administered by MCA Music Publishing, a division of MCA, Inc. All rights reserved. International copyright secured. Used by permission. Permission was also granted to print passages from *Death of a Salesman* by Arthur Miller, copyright © 1949 and renewed © 1977 by Arthur Miller. Used by permission of Viking Penguin, a division of Penguin Books USA Inc.

Dear Readers,

This book is in some ways autobiographical. I got caught in a snowstorm near the turnoff to Plain City on Interstate 70 one day when I was on my way to teach at Ohio State University. The storm grew worse and became a sleet-and-snow storm. I took the Plain City exit, figuring I would just go to Mickey D's, whose sign (golden arches) I'd just seen. Slipping and sliding all the way, trying to see, I took the road toward Plain City. Only I never found the town. I kept going and going and it never showed up! So I turned back and was forced to go on to Columbus, only to find the University was closed! A bad day for me. However, I managed to ride out the storm overnight at a friend's house. But after that, I wondered about Plain City. I began to imagine what it would be like. Then, suddenly, I pictured this wild-looking child, this girl, with carrot-colored hair, all dressed in white in the dead of winter. I saw her striding through the snow across the countryside. That vision captured me; I had to follow Buhlaire with words, describing what I saw in my head. I caught up with her with the use of prose, and found out who she was.

She is my kind of kid, probably the way I was at twelve or thirteen — intensely alone, independent, uncertain, like most kids at that age. I had a good time making her story. I grew very fond of her mother, Bluezy Sims, her aunts, and her sadly disturbed father. I liked her friend, Sandy, and the boy who follows her. I live in close comfort with my characters and see them through to the end.

I never did see the real Plain City. But I hear it's different from the one I created.

Virginia Hamilton